# SUNRISE, YEOMANS COUNTY

# SUNRISE
## YEOMANS COUNTY

*A NOVEL BY*

# MICHAEL DESCAMP

PORTLAND • OREGON
INKWATERPRESS.COM

Publisher:  Inkwater Press  |  www.inkwaterpress.com

Paperback   ISBN-13 978-1-62901-589-7  |  ISBN-10 1-62901-589-X
Kindle       ISBN-13 978-1-62901-590-3  |  ISBN-10 1-62901-590-3


1 3 5 7 9 10 8 6 4 2

## Dedications

To my wife Jackie, for support and encouragement and an occasional jab to the ribs when I was finding the story hard to finish. This book has had a gestation period of five years – half our lifetime together – and I'm glad we both feel it was worth it;

To George Van Horn at Reptile World in St. Cloud, Florida, who showed me the finer points of separating snakes from their venom;

And to Mary Rosenblum (1952-2018) – author, cheesemaker, pilot, editor and friend. You forced me to kill off some really attractive characters and to rip the guts out of my first draft of "Sunrise". You were right; it's a much better book for it.

# WINTER

## CHAPTER ONE

I CARRIED THE AFTERNOON MAIL AND A TEN-POUND BAG OF dog food outside to the back deck of my condo. The mail went on the table, a handful of dog food went over the railing, and the Canada geese in the slough below immediately stopped their racket. I always feel a little guilty, knowing I'm probably encouraging bad behavior by feeding them, but some of them are just too lazy to fly south for the winter.

I threw down another handful. They prefer Purina Puppy Chow, but almost anything I offer will shut them up, at least for a while.

I made a quick run through the mail, boning out *The Economist* and *The New Yorker* and adding their coupons to a pile of local ads for carpet cleaning, pizzas, and discount storm windows. The last item was a plain, white envelope with my name and address printed carefully across the front. One more donation plea for some worthy cause, I thought, complete with a hand-addressed envelope to give that personal appearance. I tossed it in a pile with the other junk, got a fleece jacket and a beer, and came back out to the deck. There was a fresh explosion of honking as I opened the sliding glass doors, which died down after a moment when no more Purina appeared. I opened the beer and stretched out on the lounge chair with *The New Yorker*, thinking dark thoughts about publishers and their deadlines. I was convinced they used one calendar when they wanted a project finished, another one entirely when they sent out checks.

Half an hour later the temperature had dropped and the winter sunlight had faded to a soft pink wash against the western clouds. The geese muttered; bats flicked across the sky; the marina's solitary beaver pushed his way down the slough and disappeared into a bank of houseboats. I finished the beer and headed inside to the kitchen. I'd long since given up cooking for one, but I could usually make a meal out of takeout leftovers if I was careful about how long they'd been around.

One taste of the kung pao chicken was enough. I dumped it in the garbage and turned to the pad Thai, which came off a little better. I ate standing at the counter, shuffling through the pile of mail once more before consigning everything to the trash. The faint cancellation marks on the white envelope stood out more clearly under the bright kitchen lights. I looked closer.

Georgia. Yeomans.

A sour taste rose up in my throat and it wasn't from the pad Thai.

The envelope was an old style, white commercial envelope, standard business size. On the front was my address, carefully handwritten in block letters, along with a single 'Forever' issue stamp in a Christmas theme. No return address on the front or back. I cut the envelope open and pulled out two pieces of paper. The first was a photocopy of an old news clipping:

AUTHORITIES SEEK MISSING TEACHER

The Yeomans County Sheriff's Department is seeking a missing Yeomans resident.

Charles Avery Burroughs, a teacher at Yeomans Junior High School, was last seen on Friday, August 3. School officials contacted the County Sheriff after Burroughs failed to report for work on Monday and Tuesday.

Sheriff's deputies and river patrol searched the area around Burroughs' home, a houseboat on the Altamaha River just off Airport Road and west of Highway 1A. A canoe thought to belong to Burroughs was discovered several miles downstream of the houseboat. Search efforts have been hampered by the terrain, which is wet and heavily wooded.

Anyone having information concerning Burroughs' whereabouts is asked to call the Yeomans County Sheriff's Office at 427-5100.

The second page was blank except for the words: *"We need to talk soon. I'll let you know. J."*

I found myself sitting down on a kitchen chair, breathing hard, a wash of bile in the back of my throat. I made it to the sink and stood there with my head down over the drain, and after a few minutes I got the urge to vomit under control. I picked up the letter again and stared at it, overcome by feelings of regret and shame for actions a half century in the past.

I put the letter down and walked upstairs. There had been a rash of burglaries on the island a couple years earlier, and in response I'd installed a safe in the bedroom. It was sitting on the floor in the back of the closet, in plain sight but bolted down from inside, kind of a 'fuck you' to any burglars who might come calling. Even if someone did manage to break in they wouldn't find much of value. I lifted out the contents and spread them on the bed: mortgage and investment account statements, some insurance papers, a few old pieces of family jewelry, an assortment of Confederate currency I'd collected through the years. No passport, no love letters, no will. Not much to show for a life.

I pulled out the last item—a business-sized envelope, yellowed with age—and carried it downstairs to the kitchen table. Inside was an original of the same newspaper clipping that I'd just received, this one falling to pieces from years of folding and unfolding, faded almost to illegibility. Across the bottom of the original was written, *"I miss you. Don't come back. Jenny."*

Jenny, I thought. After all these years, what do you want from me now?

## CHAPTER TWO

I WOKE UP WITH A START, BREATHING HARD FROM THE dream, tangled in the sheets and clammy with sweat. I kicked the blankets to one side and lay there in the stale air, trying to get back to sleep, but when dawn finally broke I gave up, threw on a robe against the cold, and went outside to sit on the deck.

The early morning winter sun shot through the clouds, painting Mt. Hood with muted shades of pink and blue and glinting off the metal roofs of the boathouses in the moorage. I could hear the morning flights lifting up out of Portland International upriver, and from below the condo came the low honk and gobble of geese, feeding in the shallows. I couldn't remember any details of the dark dream but I was still left with an uneasy, anxious feeling. I grabbed some sweats and my kayak paddle and headed down to the river. On the way out the door I stopped to leave a phone message for my brother Jack.

On most of my morning workouts I would kayak through the slack water along the shore, keeping a lookout for osprey and otters and doing more sight-seeing than real exercise. This morning I left the dock and headed straight out to the center of the river. For the next hour I ranged back and forth, battling upstream against the full force of the current, and by the time I reached the point of the island, where it split the Columbia River into two channels, I was dripping with sweat and shaking with exhaustion. I made the turn and pulled over into the shallows close to shore. Then I tucked my paddle up against my chest and leaned back, letting the current pull me slowly down-stream, thinking about the year I spent in Georgia as a kid and the lifelong effect it had on me.

## CHAPTER THREE

I MOORED THE KAYAK AND SLOWLY CLIMBED THE STEEP stairs back up the riverbank, trying to remember the last time I'd been to the gym, figuring that if I couldn't remember then it had been too long. I brewed some coffee, picked up the phone, and went out to the deck. Jack answered on the second ring.

"Hey, you were up pretty early, man, everything okay?"

"Yeah, couldn't sleep; bad dreams and night sweats. You free for coffee?"

"Just a sec." I heard the phone being put down, then a rustling of papers before he came back on the line. "Is this an emergency? I'm pretty tied up with faculty and end of term stuff today and tomorrow. No morning classes on Wednesday, though. How about we meet at the courthouse Starbucks about ten and I'll buy."

"Sounds good. Um..." I hesitated.

"Yeah?"

It had been a long time since we'd talked about anything important. How would I tell him what was going on with me now if I didn't understand it myself?

"Anything else?" He sounded, as usual, impatient.

"No, that's okay. It'll keep."

I put down the phone. The sun, which a few minutes before had warmed the chill morning air, drew back behind the clouds and a few raindrops spattered on the deck cover. I got another cup of coffee, pulled my lounge chair over into a sheltered corner, and watched as the rain picked up. A great blue heron sailed past the deck, landed awkwardly on the small beach below, and set about looking for fish in the shallows; an osprey circled overhead, fishing from a different perspective. The hum of the freeway gradually faded into white noise. I closed my eyes and took stock of my life.

Before I'd moved to Hayden Island, the crossing point for I-5 from Oregon to Washington State, I'd lived down in Portland's Pearl District. In the 1980s the Pearl was run down and cheap, filled with abandoned buildings and the occasional blue-collar café. I rented two spaces in a former warehouse, lived in one, and ran my family law practice out of the other. Five years later I bought a small mom and pop grocery, cleaned out the rats and roaches, and put my law practice on the street level and my apartment on the floor above. Then I put my head down and poured everything I had into the practice, and by the time I looked up again the Pearl had changed beyond recognition. Old buildings had been torn down or retooled. Vacant warehouses had become condos and restaurants and upscale shops, interspersed with parks and fountains and reclaimed wetlands that drew birds and other animals back to the area. Where before the population had tended toward vagrants and homeless people, now there were young professionals and parents and kids and dogs everywhere. As for me, I hadn't much to show for thirty-odd years of work but a paid-for building, enough money to live on indefinitely, and a law practice that I'd grown to hate.

I now realized that I'd lived in the middle of all that change but hadn't been a part of it. I really hadn't been part of life either, because even though I got good at forgetting events of the past, the past wouldn't let me go. I could never attach myself to anyone or anything that required a commitment. It was just too easy to isolate myself from companionship, beg off invitations, ignore opportunities for closeness; I could always plead too much work, too many deadlines. I had lots of business contacts but only a few friends. Romantic opportunities died for lack of nurturing. My friend Rebekkah, the closest thing I had to a soulmate of the female persuasion, once told me I had a hole in my life where living should be. I couldn't disagree.

The phone rang, jerking me out of my reverie. I looked at caller ID—Rebekkah, right on cue.

"Okay, I'm through waiting. Why haven't you called? You need to take me out dancing."

"You know that would be a mistake of biblical proportions, right?" I hadn't called because I'd been busy with a couple of research articles and trying to get some traction on the book. Perfectly adequate excuses, but Rebekkah always had the power to make me feel a little off-center and guilty, a little like a teenager.

"Oh, I just remembered, not dancing 'cause you're a terrible dancer. You can buy me dinner instead."

I groaned. "Listen, the last time I bought you dinner you finished off a twelve-ounce steak and a potato AND a side of prawns. Remember? And in between you ate half of what was on my plate. And then there was that chocolate volcano for dessert. I just can't keep up with you. I try, and then the next day I feel like a gorged anaconda. I can't eat for a week."

"Not my fault you have a weenie metabolism," she laughed. "Okay, let's compromise. How about a moveable feast? If the weather's good we can grab a bite to eat in the Pearl District and then walk off the calories. Let's say Thursday. That gives you a couple days to fast and get your stomach ready, so no excuses. Deal? Deal."

She clicked off before I could answer.

## CHAPTER FOUR

THE WEATHER WAS TYPICAL FOR THE HOLIDAY SEASON – forty degrees, wind gusts to thirty, horizontal rain whipping at coats and blowing out umbrellas. It matched my mood as I pushed through the door of Starbucks after another night of weird dreams and broken sleep. Inside the place was warm and dry and pleasantly quiet, and other than one intense guy with a book bag and an oversized laptop who had spread his office all over the handicapped table, the shop was empty.

I watched Jack through the big bay window as he crossed the park outside, picking his way around the puddles and heaps of wet leaves until he reached the huge bronze elk statue that stood, alone and majestic, in the roundabout. He stooped down to talk with the city workers hunkered beneath it and I had to smile. Cleaning the elk's undercarriage was one of Portland's holiday rituals, made necessary by another Portland holiday ritual: painting the elk's balls gold. The custom had been started in the early 1960s by kids from some of the city's elite families, but now many of those same kids were upstanding citizens, and they were 'shocked, shocked!' by such vandalism.

A beat cop stopped to join him. A short conversation, then they both laughed and the cop shrugged his shoulders: Whaddaya gonna do? The pranksters had gotten away with it again.

A few minutes later Jack slipped in the door, stopping just inside to shake the rain off his well-worn trench coat and battered brief case. He spotted me and grinned, then came over to drop the wet briefcase on the table before making his way to the counter. Brilliant but rumpled professor, I thought; it would be a caricature if it weren't true. A few minutes later he returned, set down his coffee and made quick work of his muffin, talking around the mouthfuls.

"You have no idea what it takes to get published in this market." Chew. Swallow. "No one cares about serious writing; Christ, it's all zombies and vampires. When did people stop reading the classics?"

"Only about a hundred years ago." Whenever we got together the conversation invariably turned to writing. Jack split his efforts between his poetry and his never-ending research on Winston Churchill, the subject of his most popular class at Portland State. Because of my law practice I had begun to write about child abuse and pedophilia, trying to figure out why some people were driven to such acts.

Jack finished his muffin and eyed my scone. "You going to eat that whole thing?"

I slid a piece over to him. "You probably need it more than I do. Applying gold paint on the run must be hard work, I imagine. How did you get away with it this year? I assume there was pretty good security around the statue."

Jack smiled. "No idea what you're talking about. If I did, though, I'd tell you that a well-placed fifty can cause temporary blindness during the Christmas season."

The wind blew gusts of rain and leaves against the window as we talked, and the mid-morning crowd from the court house area trickled in and gradually filled the shop. Jack finished sharing the latest piece of campus gossip and cleared his throat.

"You mentioned some dreams and stomach stuff. What's up with that?"

I hesitated for a second. We'd been brothers and friends for over sixty years but we hadn't talked seriously for a long time. Now that I had the chance I wasn't sure what to say.

"Yeah, I'm having the same weird dreams over and over. No detail, just darkness with a hint of monsters at the margins; sort of night-time panic attacks. Haven't been able to sleep lately."

Jack licked his finger and chased some crumbs around the plate. "Probably just your reaction to retirement. Think about your situation, you know, going to full-time writing without any backup? I'm not a shrink but that's a lotta change."

I nodded. "Yeah, it's not just that, though. Remember the book idea I'm working on? True crime, sort of a 'ripped from the headlines' novel about child abuse and pedophilia? I've got the characters and plot line down but I don't know if I can make the transition from academic articles to fiction. And just doing the research, the case studies I'm using for background; it's all important and intriguing but it kind of makes me sick."

"Well, if it were me, I'd look for a different story to tell. I mean, if the research affects you this way..." He broke off another piece of my scone and held it up for my approval. I nodded. A young couple wrestled a double stroller in through the front door and looked around the crowded shop for a place to sit. The father gave the laptop guy a dirty look as they went by to unload their kids at a small table by the window. Outside, the wind blew harder, plastering the large windows with leaves, bending them inward with each gust.

Jack looked at his watch. "I've got office hours and a class prep in a little while. Anything else, or...?"

"Yeah," I said. "This may sound weird, but what do you remember about Yeomans?"

Jack put his coffee down and looked at me. "What brought that up? Little dirt bag town, pretty much. What about it?"

"I mean, what do you really remember? You were two grades ahead of me; you ran around with a different crowd, a lot more freedom. What was it like for you?"

Jack took another piece of my scone, chewed in silence, his eyes closed. I drank my coffee and waited. After a moment he took a deep breath and blew it out.

"I don't know. Shit, I haven't thought about that place in what, fifty years? Let's see...I do remember I was pissed off most of the time. I mean, I'd planned to go to U of W after high school, then all of a sudden we were three thousand miles away and I didn't figure I'd ever see Washington again. Good thing there was football and booze." He chuckled. "Getting laid for the first time didn't hurt either."

"You ever feel out of place there? Afraid?"

"Naw." Jack finished off the last of the crumbs and licked his fingers. "I found some guys to run with, Judge and some others, pretty soon after we got there and everything was okay. And football, most of my friends were on the team, you know; nobody screwed with us. What are you getting at?"

"Well, remember Jenny? She and I were in the same grade? She just got in touch."

"No shit! God, that's been a long time. You went out with her, right; you and she used to hang out with Judge's brother. Del or something, wasn't it? That kid who died?"

"Dal. Yeah, we were all pretty much bookworms. We..."

"Boy, that's for sure. I remember now. You and he were always getting harassed for being weenies and pussies."

The memories came flooding back and my stomach knotted as I remembered the hazing and the fights. It wasn't just because I was a Yankee, although that was a big part of the problem because most of the kids in our school had never seen a Yankee before. No, it was the suspicion that went along with being different, any kind of different...

"I remember some guys kidded around that he and you were, you know, gay. I do remember Judge getting really pissed at one guy for saying it, beat him up, too. I didn't think you were, of course, just laughed it off. You weren't, right?" He punched my shoulder and grinned. I winced. He dropped his napkin on the plate and finished the last of his coffee.

"Okay, I gotta go pretty quick so maybe we can wrap this up. Had a checkup lately?"

"Yeah, my yearly thing at the VA. Just the typical enlarged prostate, up at night peeing a lot, nothing else."

"And Viet Nam was a long time ago; you should be able to rule out PTSD. So what else? You're not in any trouble with the law, are you? No deep, dark secrets in your past, right?"

I started to respond but he looked at his watch again and pushed ahead. Always impatient, I thought; always pressed for time. When did we stop really listening to each other?

"So, let's see, you've retired after years of doing the same thing every day. Your old routine is gone and you're trying something brand new. You're trying to write a novel and you're worried about not being successful. And you wonder why you're having some stomach and sleeping issues? Be surprising if you didn't." He leaned over and lifted the heavy briefcase up into his lap.

"I don't know what to tell you. Wish I could help, but..." He shrugged, shifting in his seat.

In my mind I could see the letter lying on the table, threatening to take me back to a time and place I'd spent most of my life trying to forget. I took in a deep breath, let it out, said nothing. Jack looked at me and stood up.

"Gotta go. Hang in there and give me a call if, you know, I can help with anything else." He clamped his hand down on my shoulder and shook it as he headed for the door.

## CHAPTER FIVE

DINNER WITH REBEKKAH WAS A MIXED BAG. AFTER EATING dim sum and walking around the Pearl we stopped at Jamison Park, me to digest and Rebekkah to take off the heels she insisted on wearing for any evening out. As usual the conversation veered toward the subject of relationships.

We sat halfway up the long, stepped ledges above the fountain. Rebekkah took off her shoes, breathed a huge sigh, and lifted up a foot for me to massage.

"Jeez, what I do for fashion. I sometimes wonder if it's worth the pain." She leaned back against the rock wall and made appreciative noises while I kneaded.

"Hey, don't change. I love the look. Seriously, you are gorgeous. You've always been gorgeous."

"Well, I was beginning to wonder about your... intentions." She hesitated. "Remember when Jack introduced us, when he did his poetry reading? That was a fun night, and afterward there were some other fun nights. I really enjoyed the dinners and the symphony and I thought it might turn into something serious. Then, what the hell, you just dropped off the edge of the earth." She pulled her foot away and stood up, paced on the ledge for a minute, then came back and sat down. She didn't offer me her foot again.

"So you call a couple times and I call a couple times but there's always something; research deadlines, winding down your practice, retirement planning, something. And you're so goddamn serious and preoccupied. I almost get the feeling you're looking over your shoulder all the time." She gave a sigh of exasperation. "You're a little more fun tonight, finally, but most of the time you act like you're miles away. Wanna share?"

"It's a long story. I'm in the middle of trying to figure it all out, myself. If you really want to know..."

"I do."

"...I'm not sure I can give you a straight answer, not right this minute. I've been having trouble with dreams, the same ones cropping up over and over. They started when I was a kid, and over the years they'd come and go. But they've gotten more intense in the last couple of years. Now I'm also having symptoms while I'm awake: nausea, panic every once in a while, kind of a low-level depression."

Rebekkah nodded, silent.

"I used to be drawn to child abuse cases in my practice; I thought I could have some positive affect on the kids' lives. Then a couple years ago I got interested in the abusers themselves. Before then it was just hating them and wishing they'd spend eternity in hell. Then

I started to wonder what made them tick. And then I got the idea of writing about them; crime fiction with an abuser, a truly evil person, as the main character. Something on the order of "Silence of the Lambs" but with a local flavor. Problem is, the more I studied these people, the worse my symptoms got. So now I've gotta make some choices. I could dig in, try to write some really great fiction, and just put up with the symptoms. Or I could just turn away from the whole thing, enjoy being retired, and hope the symptoms go away."

"Sounds like kind of a no-win to me."

"Might not have to be that way. There's someone I knew a long time ago—just got in touch—who might be able to shed some light on things. I sure hope so, anyway." I reached out and took her hand with both of mine. "What I'm trying to say is this doesn't have anything to do with you. I need to figure myself out so I can be fit for some kind of relationship."

Rebekkah looked at me for a moment, then sighed and gently pulled her hand away. "I hope you find your answers, Will. And I hope it's soon, because I'm not going to wait forever."

## CHAPTER SIX

IN THE DREAM I HAD BURROWED DOWN INTO MY SLEEPING bag, seeking warmth, leaving only a slit for my eyes. Somehow my tent had disappeared overnight, and from where I lay in the middle of the naked campsite I could see the stars overhead and shapes of trees and bushes standing against the darker mass of the forest, silent monsters in the hours before dawn. A short, insistent buzz came from somewhere in the darkness. I froze in position, remembering the sound and reviewing what I'd learned about Eastern rattlesnakes, starting with their specially adapted pupils that gave them an advantage hunting prey at night.

I forced myself to lie quietly and several minutes passed before I heard the buzz again. As far as I could tell the snake hadn't moved from its position. I closed my eyes—more memories. I remembered that the snake had pits under its snout to sense a prey's body heat and a forked tongue to taste the air and locate a victim's direction. I remembered that the Eastern rattler was one of the largest North American snakes, with an average length of about six feet. I also remembered that back in the '50s someone had killed an eight-foot specimen down in St. Augustine, just south of Yeomans. Not as venomous as, say, a coral snake—which tended to be much smaller—but capable of pumping out a lot more poison in a shorter amount of time. Its victims had a mortality rate of about thirty percent, mostly from cardiac arrest. And finally I remembered the thrill of handling one of the snakes, holding it down to extract the venom, marveling at the beauty and strength of the body beneath its beaded, multicolored skin. Jenny wouldn't come anywhere near them, couldn't even stand to look at them. She thought I was crazy.

Another buzz and I burrowed down further to escape the sound, pulling the pillow over my head, suddenly wondering what I was doing camping with a pillow. I opened my eyes to the dim light of early morning, where the trees and bushes of my dream resolved themselves into the furniture and doorways of my bedroom. I rolled over and picked up my iPhone from the bedside table, my hands shaking. Three messages in the past five minutes, all the same:

*"You have to come back now. We need to talk. jdjyeomans@gmail.com."*

I closed my eyes and half a century fell away. It was twilight and I was sitting beside Jenny on her porch glider. From the kitchen came the muted sounds of her dad's favorite radio station, along with the smell and sizzle of frying pork chops. Honeybees droned their way toward evening in the garden outside, and a soft breeze brought the scent of lilacs in through the screen. My arm was on the back of the glider, perched just barely above Jenny's shoulder. I breathed in her scent as we rocked back and forth, her old dog snoring contentedly on the floor beneath the swing. I was just about to tell her that I loved her.

I looked at the blinking message, typed in *"Where?"* and hit the send button.

The answer came back almost immediately. *"Pinehurst Nursing Home, 20 miles west of Yeomans on SR33. Room 114. Supervisor is Mrs. Jessup. She's expecting you. Come now. J."*

⌇

I'd flown the Delta red-eye to Atlanta before, but not on such short notice and not during the Christmas season. All the overhead compartment space was gone by the time I got to my seat: last row, window, next to the bathrooms. I stuffed my overnight bag down by my feet and kicked it forward to create some space, at the same time trying to avoid too much contact with my overweight neighbor whose ample arm completely covered the armrest between us. I thought about Rebekkah, wishing I'd been able to reach her instead of just leaving a voicemail.

Outside the rain had turned to a light mist and the runway lights were shrouded in fog, planes flickering past like huge silver ghosts, floating into position down the tarmac. The engines changed pitch as we lined up at the end of the runway. I leaned my head against the window and closed my eyes, hoping for some sleep, thinking of my first visit to Georgia half a century before.

# SUMMER

## CHAPTER SEVEN

"TOM, THERE'S A COW ON THE RUNWAY."

Mom hadn't raised her voice but she sounded anxious, and considering the way our trip was going, this was not a good thing. We'd driven from our little town of Shelton, Washington to Seattle, flown through thunderstorms all night, and by the time we got into Chicago everybody was tired and short-tempered and Martha had thrown up twice. Mom had had just enough time to clean her up and make sure everybody got a little something to eat before we left for Atlanta. When we arrived at nine in the morning, the temperature was already eighty degrees, and my shoes stuck to the blacktop as we walked from the terminal out to the plane for our final flight to Yeomans. Mom was enormously pregnant and her patience, which had already been stretched thin by Jack's complaints and Martha's airsickness, was at the breaking point.

I looked from my window as the plane banked around the end of the single runway. Below, I could see row after row of pine trees, broken up by areas of sand and tiny, shrub-like palms. Away in the distance was a river, curling upon itself like a bright blue ribbon dropped from the sky. I could see little cabins scattered along the riverbank and clusters of houseboats in the water, and back from the river were farmhouses and cultivated fields along country roads. The whole scene was washed in brilliant golden sunlight.

And there was the cow, standing squarely in the middle of the dirt runway.

Dad leaned across me and peered out the tiny window at the unending flat, green carpet of trees stretching out below us in all directions. Behind us Mom shifted in her seat and gave an impatient sigh. Even with air conditioning the air in the plane was unbearably humid, the fuselage was hot to the touch, and our family was beginning to smell.

"Tom! The cow!" I heard an edge of worry and a touch of anger in her voice. Dad quit counting trees and turned around.

"Ann, let's let the pilot do his job." He used his reasonable voice, the one that so often drove Mom nuts.

The plane straightened out and we flew a long pass parallel to the runway. This time we were low enough that I could see the cow clearly; it was short and brown and bony, with heavy black horns pointed forward in a V. As we flew another slow pass a man came out of a small building and walked across the runway toward the cow, waving his arms in the air. The cow looked at him for a moment, then turned and moved slowly off to the edge of the runway, across a shallow ditch, and into an adjacent field.

A few minutes later we landed and stepped down from the plane into air that was hot and wet and still. At the edge of the dirt parking lot was a battered brown station wagon. A wiry, sunburned man leaned up against its bumper, smoking a cigarette. The door to the small airport building was closed, the cow had disappeared into the shadow of a small stand of trees, and nothing moved in the blistering heat.

It was late July, 1960, and the Yankees had landed in Georgia.

## CHAPTER EIGHT

THE MAN WITH THE STATION WAGON INTRODUCED HIMSELF as Dooley. The mill had sent him to pick us up and take us someplace we could stay until our stuff arrived. Dooley drove and Dad rode shotgun; Jack and I sprawled in the wayback, behind Mom and Martha.

"These youngsters like ta swim?" Dooley asked as he leaned out the window and spat. The end of the brown stream clipped the tailfin just beyond my head. "Mill said to put y'all at the Blue Lake out north a town. Nice motel with a lake out back; might help some with the heat."

Dad said yes, that sounded good; Jack grinned and punched me in the shoulder. I lay back on the jumbled luggage and closed my eyes, willing us to just be there and have the trip over with.

The Blue Lake Motel was a row of small bunga-lows at the junction of the airport road and a state highway. All the units were low, flat-roofed buildings, painted in peeling pastels, with a graveled space out front for parking. Scattered between the units were palm trees and some grass that looked like it was losing the fight for survival in the sandy soil. We piled out of the station wagon and dragged our suitcases inside, anxious to get to the promised lake. Dad yelled a few half-hearted warnings about the water and the sun and other dangers, then he and Mom went to their own room to lie down.

The lake was shallow and absolutely clear, with a bottom of fine, white sand. Martha found an unattended beach umbrella and crawled under it with her book, and after a quick swim I laid down my towel and stretched out in the sun. The only sound in the still afternoon was the muted whoosh of cars passing by on the highway. I had just started to doze off when somebody tugged on my foot.

"Hey, Will!"

"What? C'mon, I'm trying to sleep!"

"Take care of Martha for a few minutes. I'm going to go look around."

"Better not. Mom said we're supposed to stay close."

Jack snorted. "Just do it, okay? I'll be right back."

He walked along the row of bungalows to the far end, where the motel office joined up with a restaurant next door called "The Pig." I got up and moved over next to Martha, who by now was sprawled fast asleep in the shade, her book open on the sand.

I was almost asleep when he tugged again. This time I tried to ignore him, but after a few tugs he gave my foot a kick.

"Hey, Will!"

"Geez, c'mon, leave me alone!"

"You still got your allowance?" Jack and I both earned a quarter a week for doing chores, and Jack often found creative ways to help me spend mine. Past experience had made me a little suspicious.

"Well..."

"Go get it. This gift shop in the restaurant—there's stuff in there you're not going to believe!"

By now Martha was fully awake. I realized that, whatever it was that Jack was so excited about, we'd have to include her. Granted, Mom would be upset if we all disappeared together without telling her, but she'd come unglued if Jack and I left Martha unattended. Mom had always had an unreasoning fear of water, and she timed us to make sure that we didn't go swimming until at least an hour after eating, because of cramps, she said. She conveniently ignored the fact that Martha was the best swimmer in the family.

"I'll get my allowance too," Martha said firmly. "I get to come." I looked at Jack and he shrugged. We went back to the room, retrieved our money and walked out around the motel office to the restaurant next door.

While the Blue Lake Motel was just aged and faded and charmless, The Pig looked like it was ready to fall over. It was a wide, single-story log building half covered in kudzu vines, its sagging roof was a patchwork of weathered shingles, and whatever color it had once been painted had now faded to a chalky grey. Its left side seemed to be leaning for support against the motel office. To its right was a gravel-covered drive hosting a collection of fifty-gallon drums, cut lengthwise and standing on rusted metal legs. The air around them was filled with smoke and the sweet smell of barbecued meat. An uneven porch stretched across the front of the building; a deeply trafficked groove led up the stairs and across the porch to a heavy timbered front door. Jack pulled the door open and we stepped into a dim, cool space that smelled faintly of cleaning products and cigarette smoke.

Most of the interior was taken up by restaurant seating. Along the right wall was a line of four-person booths covered in reddish naugahyde, bleached pink on the corners from the sun and sagging from years of use. The row of booths ended at a double swinging door into the kitchen. The rest of the space was filled with square tables and chairs. The tables were covered with scratched formica, the tables and chairs all had rounded metal legs, and the chair upholstery matched the booths. Behind the eating area were bathrooms and a small gift shop. The place was quiet except for the muffled sounds of voices back in the kitchen and the clink and slosh of an industrial dishwasher.

The swinging doors to the kitchen opened and a waitress stuck her head out.

"You young folks are early. We don't start servin' dinner for another hour. Y'all need anything?"

"No, ma'am," said Jack, "we're just going back to the gift shop."

The waitress surveyed us briefly and smiled. "Well, that's fine, then. You just be careful back there."

The gift shop was filled with items that were totally foreign to us: burlap sacks filled with walnuts, cellophane-wrapped boxes of fudge and pralines, and bags of fuzzy, green, boiled peanuts labeled "Goobers." There were key chains attached to various plastic animals and several tables covered with shells and starfish and small dried lizard-like creatures. On the walls were hung an assortment of rusted swords and ancient rifles and a few painted wooden signs, including one that said "Welcome to Yeomans — Your in Confederate Country!"

As we looked around an overweight boy with short hair and a bad sunburn, about Martha's age, came into the shop and went immediately over to a table near the back wall. On the table sat a wire cage, open at the top and containing several baby chicks. Next to the cage was a bowl of change and a note that said "Chicks 5 Cents — HONOR SYSTEM." I watched as he dropped a nickel into the bowl, picked out a baby chick, and left through a door in the back of the shop. Over the door was a sign that said, simply, "ALLIGATORS."

"Ooh, look, baby chicks!" said Martha. She pulled a nickel out of her pocket, dropped it in the bowl and picked out one of the chicks. Jack and I looked at each other and followed the boy.

The door led outside to a dusty clearing behind the restaurant. Directly across the clearing was a large enclosure surrounded by a six-foot wall of wooden fence and briars. We climbed a short rise of stairs through an opening in the fence and up onto a platform overlooking a shallow, green pond. A chest-high railing, with posts every foot or so, ran around the edge of the platform, and nailed to the railing was a sign that said "KEEP HANDS IN." The sunburned boy squatted down between the posts and held his frantically peeping chick out over the surface of the pond, a pond, I suddenly realized, that was filled with snouts and eyeballs and the occasional scaly tail. For a moment there was silence.

"GahDAMMit, Steven, what are you doing? Get the hell away from there this minute!" screamed a large woman as she burst through the back door of the restaurant.

The boy leaped to his feet, whacked his head on the underside of the railing, and fell back onto the platform. The chick flew from his grasp and was snatched in mid-air by an impressively sized alligator, which had launched itself straight up out of the pond, its jaws narrowly missing the boy's hand.

Martha screamed and dropped her chick. The bird scrambled down the stairs, peeping frantically, and made a break for freedom into the briars just as Mom arrived on the scene. Mom didn't wait for an explanation; she just grabbed me and Jack each by the ear and herded us back to the room, promising that we'd be in real trouble when Dad got back with the groceries. Martha followed behind, a huge smile on her face.

I had to smile too. Whatever punishment might be in store, this had been worth it.

## CHAPTER NINE

"EWG, WHAT IS THIS?" JACK SAID. "I JUST WANTED SOME eggs." He poked at a small white mound on his plate, took a spoonful and tasted, took another. "I dunno, kind of salty and buttery." He smacked his lips. "Guess it's okay."

Our waitress stopped on her way past and looked over his shoulder. "Grits, son," she said. The way she said it sounded like 'greeits.' "You never had grits? Kind of a corn meal; you eat 'em with the eggs and sausage." She filled Dad's coffee. "Where's that sweet little daughter of yours?"

"She's staying back with her mom while the boys and I go over into town and look at our new house," said Dad. Mom's pregnancy was making her hard to be around, and Dad reacted by getting antsy and finding things to do. The moving van was due to arrive any day and he wanted to drive around town, check out our new place, and, as he said, "make sure there aren't any hitches."

"Y'all be sure to come for dinner tonight, then. Chicken fried steak and blueberry pie."

We piled into Dad's rental car and headed into town, windows down, hot, humid air blowing in. Palmettos sprouted in the ditches and a dense wall of sugar pines hemmed in the highway on either side. Every so often there'd be a hole in that wall, usually a piece of land cleared back into the trees with a solitary single-story concrete block house sitting in the middle of it.

As we hit the city limits of Yeomans the two-lane highway turned into Cherry Street and took us on into the town center. To the north of Cherry were small industrial buildings and shops; to the south was a quiet, tree-lined neighborhood. The town center was a small business area along the railroad, dominated by a large, ornate Southern Pacific railroad depot.

We crossed over the tracks and drove out of town, and Cherry Street turned back into a highway. The change from town to country was sudden. One moment we were passing by homes and yards and sidewalks, listening to the sounds of lawn mowers and dogs in the hot weekend morning; the next moment there was only the hum of the tires on the hot asphalt, the scrape of crickets and the low murmur of doves in the undergrowth.

Dad kept going, past a couple of gas stations and motels and a restaurant that advertised "All You Can Eat" chicken dinners, finally pulling in at a used tire shop and garage alongside a junkyard. We sat for a few minutes before he said "I think we've seen enough" and turned the car around. I looked out the back window and watched the highway behind us, stretched out flat and straight across a landscape of sand and pines, heading for the Atlantic Ocean more than a hundred miles away.

I took a closer look as we came back through town. Near the city center and the railroad station was a cluster of buildings: the courthouse, police station, fire station, and a small library. There was also a collection of Victorian homes with wide, well-kept lawns and gardens brimming with brightly colored flowers.

Dad turned the car south before the tracks and drove through a neighborhood of smaller homes. We passed some apartment houses and the city park, the grade school, junior high, and high school, and a large football field. He pulled over when we got to the field and we watched some boys doing calisthenics and wind sprints in the early morning heat. I could hear the coach yelling at the top of his lungs, "Faster! Harder!" and was happy I had no interest at all in sports.

"Looks like your school, boys," said Dad. Jack stared at the players; I figured he was sizing them up as possible opponents. Going into his senior year he had one more season of football left, and he was angry that he'd had to leave a guaranteed spot on the team back in Shelton. He continued to watch them as we drove away, across the tracks and into a more run-down section of town.

After a few minutes Dad pulled up in front of a one-level, tan brick house. The road in front of the house was compacted dirt, two lanes wide, built up in the middle so rainwater could drain off into shallow ditches on either side. The house had a covered concrete porch and two picture windows in front and an attached one-car garage at the end of a gravel drive on the north side. To the south of the house a swampy area stretched back into the woods.

"Okay, boys. Let's take a look at our new home," Dad said, opening the front door. Jack pushed past and went through the house at a dead run.

The place had a closed-up, abandoned feeling, and the heavy air inside smelled of mildew. To my left was a family room with a hide-a-bed couch, and to my right was a large living/dining area. A long hall led from the front of the house to the back. Along the right-hand side was a single bathroom with a kitchen just beyond, along the left were two bedrooms. At the far end of the house was a small laundry room, tacked on like an afterthought. Jack stood just outside the back door and I joined him, looking at the back yard which was bare except for one small live oak tree. The brown grass lay brittle and flat in the summer heat.

"What a hole," he said.

We walked around to the front of the house and found Dad leaning against the car, a thoughtful look on his face. "Boys," he said, "we have a situation here. You're going to have a little brother or sister soon and, well, the house only has two bedrooms."

Jack and I looked at each other.

"What I mean is," Dad said, "there are only two bedrooms, and Martha and the new baby should share one of them."

"So you want Jack and me to sleep in the TV room?" I said. "With the hide-a-bed?"

Jack scowled.

"Well," said Dad, uncomfortably, "at least for the time being..."

"It's okay, Dad." I put my hand on Jack's arm and squeezed to get his attention. I didn't want him complaining; I could tell Dad was feeling bad enough as it was. "We can do it. It'll be kinda like camping out."

"Thanks, boys." Dad smiled and gave us both a hug. "We'll be moving to a bigger place soon, I promise you."

"It's still a hole," Jack said under his breath as we followed Dad back to the car.

## CHAPTER TEN

WHEN WE PULLED INTO THE MOTEL PARKING LOT MOM WAS leaning up against the front of our unit, a suitcase standing beside her. She was bent over and breathing hard, and I heard her say "bad timing" as Dad grabbed the suitcase.

"The phone number of the hospital is in on the dresser and there's some money for The Pig," Mom said. "I talked with the manager here and he'll take care of anything you need. You boys take good care of Martha and don't tease her." Dad came back and helped Mom walk to the car.

"Stay here at the motel, keep the door locked, and don't go off exploring. And no swimming. Promise."

It wasn't a request. Jack started to argue but Dad cut him short. "Promise!"

We spent the rest of the day hanging around the room and sitting out in front of the motel office, reading tourist pamphlets and swatting at mosquitos. Jack went over to The Pig and brought back some pecan pralines and boiled peanuts. The pralines stuck to their wrappers and were so sweet they made my teeth hurt. The peanuts came in a brown woven bag that looked like a little gunny sack. They were salty and soft and slimy all at the same time, and after a few bites Martha spat hers out and went to get some water. I chewed a few and gave the rest of mine to Jack.

Halfway through our dinner that night the motel manager came over to our table. "Y'all have a phone call from your daddy, in the office."

Jack jumped up and ran to get the phone. The manager looked at me and smiled. "Your daddy said everything's okay, son. Sounds like you have a new sister."

The next week was a blur. Jack and I stayed home with Martha while Mom was in the hospital and Dad was at the mill, When the movers came they emptied the van and dumped everything in the front room, saying all they'd been paid to do was to drive our stuff here. Dad couldn't get any time off from work, so he hired a couple of colored clean-up men from the mill to help me and Jack unpack and get everything put away. Jack and I worked harder than I could remember ever doing and Martha pitched in too, sorting out and carrying things that weren't too heavy for her to lift. When Mom finally got back from the hospital she was exhausted and the new baby, little Mary, spent all her time either screaming or nursing. I looked forward to Sunday like I never had before.

## CHAPTER ELEVEN

CHURCH WAS A SMALL WOODEN BUILDING WITH A LOW-pitched roof of cedar shingles topped by a simple cross. A path of crushed oyster shells, bordered by a double row of palmettos, led up to the front doors. Stuck in the sandy soil just to the right of the doors was a wooden sign with slots for interchangeable letters. Today's message read *St. Jude's. Sunday Mass at 10:30, Saturday Confession at 4:00. All Are Welcome.*

"This church stuff is crap," Jack muttered as we shut the car doors and followed the rest of the family into church. "I can't wait to be in college."

"What are you talking about? How does college change anything?"

Jack looked at me in disbelief and shook his head. "You kidding? I'm not gonna keep going to church once I'm out of the house."

I was amazed. Saturday confession, Sunday Mass,

Holy Days of Obligation; these activities were part of our family routine, as natural as getting up in the morning or going to school. Back home I'd gone to the same church for as long as I could remember. I'd never considered not going; the Catholic faith was stamped like a brand on us all; as much a part of me as my name.

"It'll never work. You'll never convince 'em."

"Don't have to; I won't be around." He smirked. "You know what else? I heard them talking last night about how the priest here isn't full time. Every fourth week he has to go over to Savannah—something about covering for some other parish. And if there isn't a priest here, there isn't a Mass. Good deal for us, huh?"

"Boys!" Dad was holding the church door open, windmilling one arm above his head to hurry us up. We raced each other to the front door and stopped just inside. To the right was a baptismal font on a stone pedestal, and to the left was the door to a single bathroom. In the middle of the open space were a couple of card tables holding cookies and a coffee service. Past the tables a set of double wooden doors led into a large main room where Mass was held. Inside, two rows of pews faced a raised altar, and to the right of the altar were two confessional booths. The windows on either side of the room were a disappointment; not the ornate stained glass that I was used to from our church back in Shelton but just pastel colored glass, propped open wide to catch the early morning breeze. Through the windows I could hear the steady hum of insects in the quiet Sunday heat.

A few curious faces turned toward us as we took our seats in the back, but they quickly snapped forward as the priest and a young boy came from behind the altar and started the ritual of Sunday Mass.

"*Intro ibo ad altare Dei,*" the priest intoned. "*Ad Deum qui laetificat, juventutum meum.*"

I will go to the altar of God, I thought; to God, who gives joy to my youth. For the first time since we arrived in Georgia a wave of homesickness rolled over me. Just a few weeks ago I'd been kneeling on the altar at St. Mark's, assisting the priest and giving the responses. I suddenly realized that, even though I complained about church, I'd feel lost without this weekly routine. In this strange new place my connection to the Church was one of the few things that felt like home.

Jack shifted on the hard, wooden pew and kicked at the padded kneeler in front of us. Dad was sitting on the other side of Mom so he couldn't reach Jack, but he gave him a warning look. After a few minutes Jack shifted again and poked me. I poked him back. The wooden seats were hard, the humid air was stifling, and the slight breeze didn't do anything but carry mosquitos through the open windows to feast on us. By this time the sweat was running down my back and my neck itched underneath my starched shirt and clip-on tie. I swiveled my head back and forth to get some relief, as well as to check out the other parishioners, and realized that we were the only family not wearing loose, comfortable clothing. I made a mental note to bring that up with Mom the first chance I got.

Baby Mary began to fuss. Mom lifted her to a comfortable position, covered her with a baby blanket, and began to nurse. At the sound of her hungry cries several women nearby had turned toward us with expressions of sympathy, but when they saw that Mom was breast-feeding their faces hardened in disapproval. I saw them whispering to one another and felt the atmosphere of the congregation cool. I was embarrassed for Mom and I could feel the shame creeping into my face. Why couldn't she use a bottle? What would these people think of us?

*"Dominus vobiscum." "Et cum spiriti tuo."*

The Lord be with you; and with your spirit.

*"Agnus Dei, qui tollis peccata mundi, miserere nobis."*

Lamb of God...The service droned on as we stood up, sat down, knelt, received Communion. I closed my eyes, remembering the cool mornings in Washington when I would walk through the big vacant lot behind our house to get to school. I remembered wading in the creek that ran through our front yard, building dams in the shallow water and playing with the spawning salmon until Dad yelled at us to let them go on their way. My world had been green and damp and cool and bug-free. I really missed it.

*"Ite, missa est." "Deo gratias."*

The mass is ended. Thanks be to God.

Thanks be to God, I thought, mentally adding my own exclamation mark.

The priest turned to face the congregation. He was a large man about Dad's age with a round, red face. He moved slowly to the center of the altar and paused for a moment, rolling his shoulders to loosen them. Then he smiled and spread his arms to take in the whole congregation, and the solemnity of the Latin Mass fell away.

"Thank you all for coming on this beautiful morning," he said. "We are blessed to be able to worship together in our family of faith. As most of you know, I'm Father Donovan." He made a few announcements about the health of several parishioners and asked for prayers for their recovery, reminded us of upcoming religious holidays, and invited everyone to stay after Mass for refreshments.

"Any visitors here for the first time?"

Dad stood up to introduce our family; Father Donovan acknowledged us and held his hands out in welcome. I looked around and saw a familiar face across the aisle—Lorraine, our waitress from The Pig. Next to her sat a boy about my age. He was tall and thin and his hair, cut in a flattop, was brown with a streak of white in the front. He wore a short-sleeved tan shirt and faded blue jeans. I caught his eye; he smiled briefly and raised his hand.

All right, I thought, maybe here's a fellow sufferer.

*"Holy God we praise Thy name, Lord of all we bow before Thee..."* Jack slipped out of the pew the moment the final hymn was finished. By the time Dad noticed and shot him a disapproving look he was already making a beeline for the back of the church and the cookies. I followed a few minutes later, got a paper cup of lemon iced tea and a plate of ginger snaps, and wandered over near the front door where the priest was talking with Dad.

"We're a mission parish here, only about twenty families," the priest said, wiping his red face and balding head with a handkerchief. His black cassock was streaked with sweat. "No need of a full-time priest. I spend most of my time at the Pinehurst nursing home over in the next county. Weekends I get pretty busy, though. Confessions here on Saturday, then I start

Sunday with 7:00 Mass back at Pinehurst. Those older folks in the home there like to get up early, I don't know why; if I had a chance I'd sleep 'til noon. Anyhow, after that it's back here for morning Mass, then afternoon mass at Beauville, down toward the coast. You might say Monday is my day of rest." He smiled and wiped his face again. "Pretty soon the Archdiocese is going to have to get me a new car. These country roads are hellacious, pardon me for saying."

When the conversation turned to Dad's work at the mill I wandered off to get some more cookies. The boy who had been sitting with Lorraine was standing by the coffee table and he smiled as I approached. I balanced my cookie plate on top of my cup and held out my hand.

"Will," I said.

"Dal," he replied.

We shook hands and looked each other over.

"Y'all are really from Washington State? That's way up in the North, right? I never met anyone from there before. Come to think of it, I never met a Yankee before."

Yankee. I remembered Dad used this word when he first told us we were moving to Georgia. He talked about slavery and how the Civil War had torn the country apart and how some people in the South were still angry because they lost the war. I remembered listening to him, thinking it was all a hundred years in the past and folks should just get over it. I also thought I'd better be kind of careful until I saw how people here, like Dal, felt about it. Time to change the subject.

"That's some, uh, interesting hair color," I said. Dal grinned as he reached up to touch the front of his hair, then bent over to show me the top of his head. There was a cross of white etched in his dark hair.

"Do it with peroxide and lemon juice," he said. "Then you hang out at the river all day; the sun turns it white. Mom like to killed me 'til I told her it was a cross and then she didn't know whether to be angry or not. She's pretty religious. She wanted me to be an altar boy and was at me and at me for the longest time. I finally said I would if I only had to do it for a year. Glad that's over with. What grade you in?"

We were both starting junior high school and there were some things we had in common: neither of us liked contact sports, and both of us were interested in band. Dal said he hoped band would take care of the phys. ed. requirement.

"Some of the kids think band is for sissies. I don't care." He lowered his voice and looked around. "I just don't want to get the shit kicked out of me on the field." He told me what to expect at school, that he lived alone with his mom, he spent a lot of time fishing and camping out on the river, and he loved to read.

"Mom, she works at the motel sometimes when she's not waitressing. Cleans out the rooms. Lots of people leave newspapers and magazines so she brings 'em home. There's *Life* and *Readers Digest* and lots of newspapers, most of 'em from up north. We got a pretty good library here, too; one of the Carnegie ones. I guess I'm about the readingest kid in my grade. Some of the other kids call me a bookworm but I don't care." He took another bite of cookie and pointed across the room.

"Looks like our moms are getting along pretty well," he said. "I just have a brother. How many in your family?"

I looked up to where our moms were sitting on

folding chairs near the front door. Martha sat between them, holding little Mary and playing with her toes. "Those are my sisters," I said, "and Dad's over there with the priest. My brother Jack's around somewhere; he's older and he hates church so he probably got out of here as soon as he could. I imagine he's out sitting in the car, waiting for us to leave." I leaned over to look out the front door. "No, there he is. Wow! Whose car is that?"

Jack was standing out in the parking lot next to a pearl-grey sedan. He was talking with an older boy in jeans and a white shirt with the sleeves rolled up. The boy was bigger than Jack, and he leaned back against the car with his hand in his pockets, his eyes half closed, looking relaxed and sure of himself.

"Oh, that. That's a 1950 Chevy Fleetline Deluxe," Dal said proudly. "Belongs to my brother Judge there. He bought it last year off a bootlegger. It was a wreck and he redid it bumper to bumper. May look stock but it's the fastest thing in the county. Round here they call it the Grey Ghost."

Judge rolled up off the car, spat in the dirt, and fished a cigarette out of a pack in his shirt pocket. He lit it, took a deep drag, flicked the match off into the parking lot, and offered the pack to Jack. Jack turned and looked back toward the church and anxiously waved the pack away.

"Judge?" I said. "Is that a kind of family name or something?"

Dal shrugged. "He's only my half-brother. His real name is Robert. Robert E. Lee, for the general, you know. Everybody calls him Judge 'cause..."

I couldn't wait for the explanation. "I gotta see this car," I said. "Mom, we're going outside. Be right back."

Mom looked up and gave a little wave before turning back to her conversation with Lorraine. She was nursing Mary again. Several of the women were looking at her with expressions of disapproval again. I caught the eye of one of the women as I went by and glared at her. She quickly looked away.

"I wish she wouldn't do that," I said to Dal as we walked out toward the parking lot. "It's embarrassing."

"Yeah, I know. Some things I wish my mom wouldn't do, too, but there's not much chance of her changing, either."

The car was painted all one color, the kind of grey you see in winter clouds. It had simple round hubcaps instead of moons, and except for the bullet grille and bumpers there was no chrome anywhere on the car. No decals, no fuzzy dice; even the hood ornament was gone. It looked clean and it looked fast. Jack and Judge had the hood up and were leaning over into the engine compartment. Judge pointed inside and said something about a carburetor; Jack looked and nodded and made appreciative noises. He'd been in love with cars by way of magazines for several years, even though he wasn't yet old enough to get his license. He and Judge ignored me and Dal, and after a few minutes the two of us walked back toward the church.

"What are you doing after?" Dal asked.

"Going out to The Pig for breakfast. You?"

"Might see you there. Mom's going to work the afternoon shift and she likes to get in early to help set up."

Mom and Lorraine were still admiring Mary when we came back inside the church. Dad was still talking with Father Donovan, but now there was another man standing with them. He was tall and slim and wore a suit despite the heat, and he rested his hand on Dad's shoulder as he talked. Dad was leaning in to listen, but when he saw us he straightened up and waved me over.

"This is Mr. Burroughs, Will. He's the band teacher and works with the Scouts. We've been talking about the band program. I think you might be interested."

Mr. Burroughs took my hand in both of his and shook it.

"Good to meet you, son; you're in good company here." He smiled, reached over, and put his arm around Dal's shoulder. "Dal here sat in on class at the end of last year; he's probably my next clarinet star." Dal gave a sheepish grin and dipped his head; a little color crept into his face.

"C'mon," said Mr. Burroughs, "don't be modest. You're gonna help us win State this year. And don't forget I've got a couple scholarships for Band Camp down at Miami." He gave Dal a hug, shook my hand again, and asked me to check in with him after school started in the fall.

After he left I looked around. Mom and Lorraine were packing up the baby and heading toward us with Martha in tow. Through the front doors I could see Jack and Judge leaning up against the Chevy. The ladies of the Altar Guild moved about, picking up paper cups and plates and salvaging the remaining cookies. I grabbed a couple of ginger snaps for the ride home and turned to say goodbye to Dal, but he was already out the door.

# CHAPTER TWELVE

THE LATE SUMMER AFTERNOON AIR WAS HOT AND HEAVY AS damp flannel. Earlier there had been a flush of rain; now the ground steamed and mosquitos swarmed up out of the ditches. I lay against the trunk of the oak tree in the back yard, swatting away the bugs and taking advantage of the tree's scant shade. Every few minutes I changed position to avoid the red ants that marched in columns through the sparse grass and sandspurs.

I was reading through my new copy of *Mad Magazine* for the third time. Dal had introduced me to *Mad* and had shown me the only newsstand in town that carried it. Mom and Dad didn't like the magazine. They called it crude and trashy, and Mom had confiscated it the first time she caught me reading it. I was more careful the next time I bought one, and since Dad worked late most nights and Mom was busy taking care of Mary and bossing Martha around, I'd been able to read it without getting caught again.

I changed my position against the tree, scratched a new mosquito bite, and squashed a particularly big ant that had crawled onto the magazine cover. I was bored; the start of school was still a week away, I hadn't seen Dal for days, and Jack was almost never home. Lately he'd been spending more and more time with Judge, either riding around in the Grey Ghost or hanging around downtown at the garage where Judge worked on the car. Hanging out with Martha was out of the question. Even if I'd wanted to, which I didn't because she was just my little sister, she was so busy helping Mom with housework and with little Mary that she wasn't available. Mom kept her on a short leash and Martha hadn't met any kids her age that she could play with. She wasn't at all happy being second in command of the household chores and she let Mom know it, often and in a loud voice. And she *really* hated it when Jack and I called her "Martha, Queen of the House."

A door slammed and I could hear Martha resuming her latest argument with Mom. I knew she would eventually give in and do what Mom wanted, but in the meantime I was really getting tired of listening to them.

The shadows lengthened as the sun pushed further to the west. I moved around the tree trunk to stay in the shade, and as I turned another page I heard the front screen door slap shut and new voices inside the house. For a moment Martha stopped her whining.

"He's out in back," I heard Mom say. "You can go on through." There was the sound of footsteps coming down the long hallway, then the back door opened and

Dal stepped down into the yard. He was followed a moment later by a girl. She had a wary expression.

"Will, this is Jenny."

Jenny walked toward me, stopped a few paces away, put her hands on her hips and looked me over. Dal didn't continue the introduction; he just stood over to one side, watching. There was an awkward silence as Jenny and I studied each other.

She was almost as tall as I was, with brown hair cut shorter than I had ever seen on a girl. She had a dark tan and a splash of freckles across her nose and down each cheek. She wore khaki shorts, a checked shirt with the sleeves pushed up above her elbows, and tennis shoes without socks. Only one of the shoes was tied. She didn't say anything, just stood there with her hands on her hips, looking at me and smiling. Dal shifted his weight from one foot to the other and looked nervous. I finally decided hell, might as well get this out of the way, and stretched out my hand.

"Hi, I'm Will."

After a moment she took my hand. Her grip was soft and warm but it was firm, too. I could feel some callouses.

"Will, huh? Dal tells me you read a lot."

The remark was so unexpected that I had to laugh. I looked at Dal. He shrugged self-consciously.

"Yeah, well, remember you said you had one of those Carnegie libraries up North," he said. "We've got one here, too, remember?"

"You can let go now."

I coughed and dropped Jenny's hand. She stepped back and looked at me and her grin got bigger.

"You like readin' to little kids?"

"Yeah, I guess, I don't know. I have a little sister," I said lamely.

She dug in the pocket of her shorts and handed me a crumpled piece of paper. At the top were the words, *Yeomans County Library Reading Night*. Below that, 'Back to School' and 'Get a Head Start on Reading.' Then there was a list—*Children's Books to Take Home*—with some of my old favorites: *McElligott's Pool*, *The Tawny Scrawny Lion*, and *The Cat in The Hat*. There were a few I didn't recognize, including a new one by Dr. Seuss called *Green Eggs and Ham*.

"The library does this ever' year before school starts, 'cause a lot of these kids don't read too good. I been after Dal to come and help. How about you?"

I looked at Dal. He shrugged and nodded.

"Okay," I said, "I'll just, um, check with my parents. I don't see why not."

"Seven o'clock," said Jenny, already on her way across the yard. She didn't look back.

For a minute Dal and I stood in silence. It was the same silence you get just after the storm passes through and you're looking over the damage.

"Friend of yours?" I asked.

"Jeez, I've known her ever since the first grade. She likes to read so we talk a lot, you know. Her dad's the biology teacher so you might be in his class..."

"No, what I mean is, is she special? A girlfriend?"

"No, no, not that way, I mean we like a lot of the same things but, uh, no." His voice trailed off and he blushed.

I looked again at the notice. Reading would start promptly at seven, older kids should get there on time so they didn't keep the younger ones waiting, refreshments would be provided. I suddenly realized I hadn't eaten all afternoon and I was starving.

"Jack's out tonight. Want to stay for dinner? Might's well—it's a long walk to your house and back."

"Okay, sure. Mom is working late so she won't have dinner ready anyhow."

I knew his mom sometimes brought home food from The Pig, but I didn't know whether it was leftovers from the kitchen or stuff people hadn't eaten. He only mentioned it once and seemed kind of uncomfortable when he did, so I didn't press him about it. I checked with Mom about dinner plans and she said it was okay for Dal to stay. Then we spent the next half hour throwing rocks at a family of frogs in the ditch and talking about girls and school.

"Jenny's the oldest kid in our class and I'm the youngest so there's no way she could be my girlfriend. Even if I wanted that, you know." He reddened a little once again. "But I like her. She and I are the only ones I know who really like to read. Some of the kids give us crap, call us bookworms. Sometimes they call me a pussy. She and I both get good grades but we don't talk much about it. It's kind of hard to fit in if you look too smart."

As soon as Dad got home from work, Mom and Martha put dinner on the table. Dad was pleased that we were going to the library; Mom said that if there was a Carnegie Library then it was the only good thing about 'this godforsaken place.'

"Now, dear," Dad said.

"Well, it's true," Mom said.

Martha smiled at Dal all through dinner. Dal

insisted on helping her clear the table and would have pitched in to do dishes if I hadn't dragged him out the door. As we were leaving Martha hit me with, "So why don't you help, like Dal?" I couldn't get out fast enough.

## CHAPTER THIRTEEN

THE SWEET, HEAVY SMELL OF CLEMATIS FOLLOWED US AS WE kicked our way through the fallen leaves in Cracker Davis Park. At the end of the park was a narrow strip of Victorian homes. As we made our way between two of them and out to the sidewalk I heard a shout and Judge's car shot across the intersection in front of us, Jack's head and arm sticking out the front passenger window. The early evening light slanted flat through the trees and reflected off a beer can in his hand. His head was thrown back, his eyes were closed, and he was doing a Rebel Yell at the top of his lungs. He'd gotten pretty good since he started hanging around with Judge, but Mom told him to keep it down at home, at least when Dad was around. She said it got on his nerves.

The Grey Ghost disappeared around the corner. We crossed the highway and walked past the city hall, the court house, the fire house and police station, all built the same: huge granite blocks and carved wooden doors and delicate stained-glass windows, with marble stairs leading from their front doors down to a flower-bordered walk.

The library was a block further down the street, at the back of a narrow lot and tucked away from the other city buildings. It was only one story tall with a half-sunk basement, almost hidden from the street by a thick tangle of live oaks and palmetto scrub. A path of paving stones led across a sandy lawn up to the library's entrance. The evening light was fading, but as we walked up the front steps I could see cracks in the foundation and the red brick walls. A plain marble slab sat above the doors, chiseled with the words, "Public Library, Est. 1899."

"Not so much of a place, huh?" said Dal. "I don't come here too often. The school library's got most everything I need. 'Cept just before school starts they have this reading get-together for the little kids, and Jenny's been at me to do it this year, so..." His voice trailed off as we picked our way up the steps between clutches of moms and their children.

Inside the library the lighting was dim and the air smelled slightly of mildew. Except for a small office by the front door and bathrooms over in the back corner, the place was one large room. Books were stacked on tall shelves along each wall. There were additional aisles of books in the back, and in the center of the room rows of wooden tables were illuminated by wide, shaded lamps that hung down from the high ceiling. The tables were filled with children, parents, and a few older kids. When Jenny saw us she left her table and came over.

"Almost gave up on y'all. Here, Yankee, I saved you a new Dr. Seuss so you wouldn't have to read the same old stuff." She handed me *Green Eggs and Ham*, and introduced me to a couple of boys who looked to be about six years old.

"This here's the Odum twins, Dru and Duane. Boys, say howdy to Mr. Letour." The boys ducked their heads and mumbled. "Mr. Letour came here from way up North to go to school," she continued. "Tonight he's gonna work with you on your reading, help you out with some of the hard words. Y'all speak up when you read for him, okay? He might be a tad hard of hearing." She gave me a wink and turned back to her table, where two little girls smiled shyly up at me, their hands folded politely in their laps. By now there was only one book left on the reading table, *The Tawny Scrawny Lion*. Dal picked it up with a sigh. "That's what we get for being late," he said. "Dibs on your book when you're done." He headed off to join a group of kids and parents near the back of the room.

Duane and Dru worked their way slowly through *Green Eggs and Ham* while I looked around at the other kids. In spite of the heat most of the boys were in coveralls and long-sleeved shirts buttoned to the chin, and all the little girls wore print dresses. Everyone was quiet. Usually when kids this age got together the boys bumped and pushed each other and the girls talked and giggled, but tonight everyone just took turns, waiting for their chance to read like it was some sort of treat.

***

Over the next hour I grabbed more books for the boys and made a show of paying attention to them, but I was listening with only half an ear; my real focus was on Jenny at the next table over. Sometimes she caught me looking at her and gave me a smile, but for the most part she was all business. I watched as she leaned forward on her tanned arms and scratched the inside of her leg with the other foot, and sometimes she would catch her lower lip between her teeth as she concentrated on the girls' progress. Dal had said he wasn't her boyfriend...

"'Scuse me." One of the brothers was tugging on my sleeve. "'Scuse me, sir, we're done with this'n." I looked around. We'd finished off everything on our table and the ones nearby.

"We're gonna have to wait a minute 'til somebody finishes another book," I said. The boys sat patiently, waiting. I realized I'd been with them for more than an hour but I didn't know anything about them.

"So where do you two live? Any other kids at home?"

They perked up and both started talking at once. They told me they lived in a small town called Sasser Crossroads, up past the mill on the river. Their daddy worked in the woods, cutting down trees and hauling them in his big rig. Sometimes they got to ride with him if he came past the house on his way back to the mill. They shared a .410 shotgun they got for their birthday and last year Duane shot a turkey with it, they knew about a special place in the river where the catfish hid, and once their daddy caught a huge lunker there with his bare hands. They had a dog and a little sister.

"How about school?" I asked. "What grade are you in?"

"Well, sir, we' just startin' this year," one of them answered proudly. "That's why Mama brung us tonight, so we can get some books to take home. We ain't got but one or two up t' the house."

"Do your parents read to you a lot?"

"Naw, just Mama does some. Daddy don't read. Mama says we need to learn how, else we'll end up..." His brother poked him hard. He shut his mouth and stared down at the desk. They both sat for a moment in silence until Jenny walked over, her two little girls trailing along behind her.

"If y'all are done, I got an idea." She held out *The Cat in The Hat*. "Girls, sit with these Odums and read together for a few minutes." We moved a little away from the table and watched as they hunkered over the book, the boys reading and the girls listening and helping out with some of the words. Jenny put her hand on my arm.

"Thanks for coming," she said. "Some of 'em need help to get started. Y'all set for school?"

"Yeah, I guess so." I thought about facing a whole new set of kids and teachers, in a place where I didn't know the rules. "But I just got here, I'm totally new, and you and Dal are the only two people I know." Jenny nodded. "Maybe if I have questions I can ask you for help for a little while 'til I get settled in?"

She grinned and patted me on the arm. "You're okay, Yankee. Y'all helped out here tonight. We'll both of us watch out for you."

## CHAPTER FOURTEEN

7:30 ON SATURDAY MORNING; THE LATE SUMMER SUN HAD already pushed the temperature above eighty degrees and my shirt was soaked through. I stopped pushing Paladin, our trusty Briggs and Stratton lawn mower, long enough to fish a red bandanna out of my jeans and wipe my face. I'd named the lawnmower after my favorite television hero: Paladin, the star of "Have Gun, Will Travel." Jack and I watched the TV show every week. Richard Boone was Paladin, dressed in black from his hat to his boots. He was a gunslinger with morals, doing his best to tame the savage land of the American West. In most of the episodes Paladin found himself in some strange and dangerous place, threatened by evil, trying to right some wrong. As a Yankee kid in deep South Georgia, I could relate.

Paladin's business card had the silhouette of a chessboard knight and the words, "Have Gun, Will

Travel." Our business card was a little less exciting: "Have Lawnmower, Will Travel," with our phone number printed underneath. Somehow it seemed right to me that the lawnmower be named after our Saturday morning hero. I hadn't shared this decision with Jack, but then I was the one who spent the most time with the lawnmower.

I crossed over the railroad tracks and pushed Paladin along a gravel walk into the park on my way to my first lawnmowing job, a big apartment complex over near the school. The park was about four blocks long, with rhododendrons and magnolia trees and huge oaks towering over the lawn. Just inside the entrance was a public swimming pool—public, that is, for whites. There wasn't any sign that said WHITES ONLY, but I'd never seen a colored person in the pool. People seemed to take this for granted. Nobody talked about it; that's just how things were. We'd only been in Georgia a short time and already I'd gotten used to the three separate bathrooms at Linnton's Rexall (men, women, and colored), and the segregated drinking fountains at the downtown Winn Dixie.

As I passed the pool I could see the lifeguards inside the chain link fence, setting out chairs and horsing around. Just after we got here Jack had come over to the pool, talked with some other kid, and landed a job the same day. He was there now, standing by the bathhouse and talking to a girl, touching her arm. She squealed and laughed and swatted at him, pushing him away. I envied him; we'd only been here a couple weeks and already he'd found his place on the social ladder.

I waved and called out but he turned and walked away behind the bathhouse.

I wrapped my bandanna around my head to protect myself from mosquitos and started out again for the apartments. I'd left home early, figuring about half an hour for the trip, but Yeomans didn't have many sidewalks in this part of town and it was slower going than I'd expected. Paladin's wheels were small and the carriage rode low to the ground; I scraped along through the gravel and the ruts, pushing up a cloud of dust to accompany the cloud of mosquitos around me. I thought about the bottle of 6-12 repellent I'd forgotten to bring. I also thought about Jack and cursed, because to some degree this Paladin adventure was his doing.

I rounded the corner at Tenth and Orange and the Eden Roc apartments stretched out in front of me for a full block—two-story townhouses with tiny concrete porches and no eaves, all painted the same weathered white, baking in the humid sunlight and surrounded by a weed-choked lawn. I pulled Paladin up on the edge of the property and sat, then jumped up and spent a few minutes swatting away the fire ants. I looked at the back of the business card to verify the address and thought grim thoughts about my brother. His role in the lawn-mowing scheme was that of organizer and manager, the same as always. When I'd complained about getting paid less than he did, even though I was doing more of the actual work, he reminded me again of the "three-legged stool" concept of business that Dad had taught us.

"Okay, look. The things we need here are Capital, Management, and Labor. Dad fronted us the money for the mower so there's the Capital taken care of. I'm doing all the really difficult Management stuff like getting the cards printed, looking around to see what buildings have crummy looking lawns, talking the owners into hiring us. So now all we have to worry about is Labor..."

I swatted a mosquito and opened up the brown bag lunch Mom had packed. Inside was a peanut butter and jelly sandwich, an apple, and a mason jar full of water from our sink at home. Mom didn't trust water from a hose because this was South Georgia, for goodness sake, and you could never tell. I took a few bites of the sandwich, washed them down with a mouthful of water, and pushed the bag and jar up under a palmetto bush for later.

I sat on the curb for a minute and thought some more. I was glad that Jack had set up the business and I had to admit that he was a lot more outgoing than me, better at meeting people and better at selling stuff. Besides, there didn't seem to be any other jobs available. From everything I'd seen so far most labor, like lawn mowing, was done by colored people. Still, I was pissed at him for taking me for granted and pissed at myself for not demanding more money.

Bottom line, though, I was a Yankee kid in the Deep South. Everyone else except me seemed to belong, and every time I opened my mouth I branded myself as an outsider. So on the plus side, mowing lawns was my way to fit in, to become invisible in this strange new place. If I kept my head down and just pushed Paladin around, that was as good as having a suit of armor. From a distance I was just another kid, working in the heat of an August Saturday morning.

I got up from the curb. The sun was already well up into the cloudless blue sky and I knew the day wasn't going to get any cooler.

# FALL

# CHAPTER FIFTEEN

FIRST DAY OF SCHOOL, AND MOM HAD MADE JACK AND ME promise to walk with Martha and get her to her homeroom. The three of us jumped the drainage ditch behind our house and picked our way between the heaps of sawdust and wood trim in the cabinet shop's lot. The sawdust had a sweet, pitchy smell and stuck to my fingers when I picked it up. A small trash burner smoldered in one corner of the lot. On bad days its smoke drifted over into our yard, and Mom complained the smoke got on the laundry that she hung out to dry. Dad called it the "smell of commerce," which was also what he called the rotten egg odor on his clothes when he came back from the mill each day. He said we shouldn't complain because smelling like sulfur told us he still had a job. Mom just rolled her eyes and made him change on the back porch before he came inside.

Martha was in a foul mood this morning; I could

hear her muttering under her breath, heard the words "dammit" and "slave." I didn't usually get involved with issues between her and Mom but this time she sounded really angry and hurt.

"What's the deal?" I asked.

She sniffled and wiped her nose. "It's Mom," she said. "Jeez, I just can't get any time for myself to just read or play or just hang around like you and Jack. If she doesn't need help with Mary then it's dishes, or folding laundry, or something else. I don't know why she doesn't ask you two to do some things around the house."

We rounded the corner of the cabinet shop and walked across the street. Jack pulled ahead, yelled back a quick *see you there*. Martha trudged along, kicking rocks out of the way with an occasional curse. I slowed up a little so I didn't leave her behind, but I didn't have any answer to her question. I wasn't really sure she expected one. I had never thought about doing housework. I figured my job was to mow the lawn and weed our small front garden and to tackle heavy projects with Dad and Jack, if there were any such projects. Housework just wasn't something that guys *did*.

We crossed over the railroad tracks that ran between the cabinet shop and the park. The railroad ties were soaked with creosote and the thick, oily smell, along with coal smoke from a recent train, reminded me of the logging operations back in Shelton. A warm morning breeze blew up from the south along the tracks, carrying with it the smell of the nearby stockyards.

We stepped into the park and walked along between large clumps of rhododendrons and magnolias. The swimming pool was still full, but the lounge chairs and throwable life preservers had been taken in for the season, and the falling oak leaves had already begun to blanket the water's surface. In the middle of the park were a basketball court and two tennis courts. At the far end, where the park ran up against the school grounds, was an area with swings and slides and a merry-go-round. We stopped for a minute in the shadow of the trees, looking out toward the school.

"Are you scared?" Martha asked.

"Of what?"

"Of school, of being here, of everything. I don't know any kids and I don't know any teachers and I don't even know for sure what classes I'm going to get. Honest to God, I can't even understand people when they talk. Everything's so different."

I tried to put my arm around her shoulder but she shrugged me off and went on ahead. I caught up with her at the edge of the park and we stood together, looking across the street at the school. Off to our right was the gym, sitting down in a bowl beside the football field. To the left was a cluster of one-story, unpainted wooden buildings, and directly ahead was a newer complex of concrete and glass. I put my arm around Martha's shoulders.

"Got your schedule? You know where your rooms are?" I checked my own bag to make sure I hadn't forgotten anything. "You OK?"

She took in a deep breath and nodded, and together we headed across the street.

## CHAPTER SIXTEEN

I WALKED INTO HOME ROOM JUST BEFORE THE LATE BELL. There was one empty seat left, next to the window way in the back of the room, and as I walked toward it I felt the eyes of the other kids on me. The teacher was standing in front of her desk, tapping her foot, waiting for the class to quiet down and for me to take my seat. She wasn't smiling. Her name was written up on the blackboard in a perfect cursive script: Miss MacDonald. She was rail-thin and just a little taller than Mom, with short brown hair that flared outward just above her ears like a helmet. Across her desk lay a heavy, steel-edged wooden yardstick. It had a well-used appearance.

She picked it up and whacked it once on the desk to get our attention. When she was satisfied with the silence she read the home room roster: Elwood Burris, Clayton DeKalb, Cobb Gwinnett, T. Beau Johnson. When she came to my name she stopped and looked me over. The kids turned in their seats and did the same. Off in the distance a dog barked and a car horn sounded, then after a silence that seemed to last forever she took up the roll again. I slid down as low as possible and looked out the open, screenless window.

The view was bleak. Next to us was another wooden classroom, separated from ours by a dry yard filled with sandspurs and palmetto shrubs. There was no grass and the only tree in sight was a stunted live oak. Its lower branches were bare; stripped clean, I figured, by students with nothing else to do. I sat in the heavy, moist air, closed my eyes, listened to the roll call and thought about escape. The bottom of the window was near the floor; I could wait until Miss MacDonald's back was turned, then throw a leg over the low sill, drop to the ground, and take off for home. I hated being indoors when the weather was like this. Just this last weekend Dal had talked about getting some inner tubes, drifting down the Altamaha. Maybe Jenny could come along; I could ask her…

"Mr. Letour!"

I jumped and opened my eyes. She had finished the roll and was looking directly at me.

"Yes, Ma'am?"

"You're new here this year. Where's your family from?"

I had been hoping to move quietly from class to class, unnoticed, at least until I got my bearings. No such luck, it seemed.

"Washington, Ma'am," I admitted.

Up until now the other kids had been settling in, stowing away books and pencils, passing notes and poking at each other. When I answered there was a collective intake of breath, and then whispers ran around the room.

"Washington? Dang!"

"Yankee!"

"Nigger lover!"

There was some stifled laughter before Miss Mac-Donald slapped the yardstick down on the desk. The sudden crack silenced the room. "Class, I will remind you that Mr. Letour is a guest in our school and you will treat him with respect. I will also remind you not to use that word in my class." She glared at the kid who'd called me a "nigger lover" and waited to see if anyone else had something to say. When no one did she turned and walked over to the blackboard, reached up above it and rolled down a heavy canvas map.

"Mr. Letour is not from Washington, DC. Washington, DC is above us, on the right. His Washington is in the Pacific Northwest, cattycorner from us." With her yardstick she traced the distance from Georgia in the lower right-hand corner of the map to Washington State in the upper left. She talked about the differences between our two states; that Georgia grew peaches and tobacco and cotton, Washington produced timber, grain, and apples. She made the point that Washington was still only a territory at the time of the Civil War and didn't have much to do with the conflict.

Then she turned to school-related issues: school rules, class schedules, and upcoming events, most of which had to do with sports. I did my best to listen, but each time I looked up from my desk there was the same kid, short and stocky and missing a front tooth, staring at me from a couple of rows over. He'd catch my eye and mouth the words "nigger lover." Then he'd poke the kid next to him and the two of them would laugh under their breath.

When the bell rang I hung back until everybody else had left, then I picked up my books and went to find my locker. As soon as I came out of the room three of the kids from class got in my way. The one with the missing tooth pushed himself in front of me, blocking my path. He stood for a minute with his fists clenched, his face twisted with anger. He cleared his throat, looked down and spat on my shoe. His friends hooted and punched each other and urged him on. He looked back up at me.

"You and your fam'ly, we don't want y'all here," he said in a low, menacing drawl. "Don't matter which Washington. Y'all 're from the North. You Yankees..."

"Clayton Dekalb!"

He stopped and turned. Jenny stepped out of the crowd with Dal right behind her, looking angry. She stood for a minute with her arms crossed, then she walked forward and planted herself in front of the kid. He stepped back to get out of her way.

"Clayton, what're you doing?"

Clayton fidgeted for a moment, looking around for support. By now his friends had melted into the crowd. He took a deep breath.

"He shouldn't be here; he's a Yankee. I'm gonna teach..."

Jenny cut him off. "Clayton, shut up and listen to me. You're not going to teach anyone anything. You're a miserable shitweasel..." Clayton's jaw dropped and his face got red. He started to reply but Jenny held up her hand. "I kicked your ass in the seventh grade and I kicked your ass in the eighth grade and I can do it again. Now get on outta here and leave him alone."

There were snickers from the students, including Clayton's followers, and back in the crowd someone said, "Hooee, she sure told him!" Clayton turned, gave me a look of pure hatred and leaned closer. "I'll git you," he said, under his breath. He stalked away without looking back.

The other students wandered off. I was shaking with tension and I realized I had been holding my breath. When I turned to thank Jenny she had already left.

I met up with Dal after third period and together we walked over to the cafeteria. He didn't see anything unusual about how Jenny treated Clayton.

"I've known her all my life and I know she hates to see people gettin' pushed around. She's not scared of anything. Plus she's really smart, smarter 'n me, even." I saw a flash of pride and then a little hint of embarrassment on his face.

"I guess she and I are maybe the smartest kids in our class," he continued. "We don't show it much 'cause you get labeled as stuck up and a bookworm. And when that happens kids like Clayton pick at us."

By now we'd reached the wide concrete steps in front of the new Administration Building. Kids were backed up and shoving at each other around the front door, trying to be first into the cafeteria so they could grab some extra playground time before afternoon classes started. I stayed on the lookout for Clayton. If this was what I had to expect from school then it was going to be a long year.

The cafeteria was a sea of chairs and folding tables, bordered by the food line along one side and the bathrooms and offices along the other. I looked around and saw Jenny sitting by herself over in the far corner. Dal picked up a metal tray and slid it along the food line; I followed along behind. The servers piled the same food on every plate and urged us all to move along. The only choice I got to make was what to drink—a carton of milk or a plastic glass of something brown that Dal said was iced tea. The day outside was already hot and the cafeteria was stifling; I went with the tea. When I got to the end of the line I looked around for someone to pay but there wasn't any cashier.

Jenny looked up as Dal and I approached, gave us a nod, and went back to her food. I sat down across from her and took a good look at my plate.

Most days back in Shelton I brought a sack lunch to school, because it saved money and Mom thought it was healthier. When I did get to buy lunch the food was pretty simple—spaghetti, meat loaf, some vegetable like mashed potatoes or string beans, and maybe an apple for dessert. Here nobody carried a sack lunch and everybody ate for free. And the portions were huge. My plate of food reminded me of a holiday dinner with one difference: I didn't recognize anything except for the fried chicken.

I poked at some of the food for a minute, pushing it around for a better look, and suddenly realized that Dal and Jenny were staring. They looked at each other and laughed.

"Okay," I said. I separated the contents of the plate into individual piles. "What is all this?"

Jenny shook her head. "This green stuff is collards. Kind of like spinach and you put vinegar on it. 'Course you know peas; these are black eye peas. These here—hush puppies to go along with your fried chicken. And you better not tell me you don't know fried chicken. Y'all can spice it all up with a little pepper sauce. This here McIlhenny's is the best. They cook it up over to Avery Island on the coast." She leaned in, grinning, and shook half a dozen drops on my chicken. "Take a taste."

I cut off a chunk of the chicken, popped it in my mouth and started to chew. In a second my tongue was on fire. My throat closed up, my nose started to run, and tears poured down my cheeks. I grabbed the glass of iced tea and took a huge gulp to wash the pepper away but it just made things worse, like swallowing a mouthful of liquid sugar. I choked everything down and sat, breathing hard, eyes and nose running like a river. I looked up to see Dal shaking his head. Jenny stared at me, a look of amusement and pity on her face.

"Oh, Yankee," she said, "you got a lot t' get used to."

# CHAPTER SEVENTEEN

I MET UP WITH DAL AND JENNY ON MY WAY TO BIOLOGY, THE last class of the day. We pushed our way through the tide of students that flowed along the row of older classrooms: single-story, unpainted buildings weathered grey with age. Each building stood a few feet off the ground, supported by wooden pilings. The empty space underneath was wrapped in chicken wire. Dal said it was to keep out stray balls and kids.

The biology classroom sat alone out on the edge of the school grounds, looking like a little house trailer without wheels. We found our seats just as the bell rang and Mr. Yeomans walked in. He crossed the room to his corner desk and looked over his classroom: six double desks lined up against one wall and stretching the length of the trailer. I stared across the room at the opposite wall where gnarled oak branches stretched from floor to ceiling, supporting a tangle of plants and flowers. Some plants were thick and fleshy, many of them were orchids, one had a single, tiny white flower at the end of a delicate stalk. One of the plants even looked like a small pineapple. Streamers of Spanish moss wove around and between shallow wire- and glass-fronted cages. Along the floor and running the length of the wall was a deep, metal pan filled with dirt and rocks. The air in the trailer was as warm and moist as a jungle.

Mr. Yeomans sat down on the corner of his desk and leaned forward, silent for a moment. Then he said, "For what it's worth, the school district had to make a decision between more money for sports or a new biology classroom. I held out for sports. That wall you're looking at? You can't tell from here but it's basically holding up the roof on that side. It's my best teaching tool and it took me fifteen years to cultivate. No way was I going to let them tear it down."

He walked over to the plant wall. "You've probably heard from other students that this class is different. I've heard some say 'peculiar.' Don't you worry; we'll get all the basics covered so you can pass the tests and move on to next year's class. Today I want to start you out with a core idea that runs through biology, which is the following. All species that are still around on this earth are here because they were able to adapt to their environments. We need to be aware of that so we humans don't get in their way. Another core idea is that living things survive and thrive best when they work together." He looked over at Jenny and gave me a passing glance. "That includes humans." Jenny squirmed in her seat. I wondered if he'd heard about the run-in with Clayton.

"For example," he continued, "think about the difference between mistletoe and wild orchids. Any of you seen clumps of mistletoe up in the swamp oaks? Maybe you harvest it around Christmas, sell it for decorations?" Some of the boys nodded. "Well, mistletoe's a parasite. Gets up in that oak tree and attaches itself and just sucks the life right out of it. It stays there long enough it'll kill the whole tree. But your wild orchids and Spanish moss, they perch up in that same tree and get along fine with just a little rain and some food blown in on the wind. They don't damage the tree. They don't ask anything from it but a place to hang and be left alone."

For the next half-hour he walked along the living wall, explaining how its many different plants fit into their special place in the forest. He described the life cycles of orchids and the many kinds of air plants. He pointed out that the stringy, delicate Spanish moss was in the same family as the huge stag horn bromeliad he had hung up near the ceiling. He explained that even the small pineapple-looking plant, which was, in fact, a pineapple, belonged in this group. At the end he said, "Next time you're out in the woods, or even in your own yard, remember to look closely at the plants and animals around you. It will help you to understand the glory of God's creation."

There wasn't a sound in the room when he finished. He looked us over for a minute and then asked, almost as an afterthought, "Any of y'all poetry fans?"

Jenny sighed. "Jeez, poetry again," she whispered,

just loud enough for me to hear. One of the girls raised her hand shyly and put it down as soon as she realized she was the only one. Mr. Yeomans didn't seem to notice. He walked over to the wall of plants, cradled one of the delicate flowers in his big hand, and recited:

*"Oh, flower in the crannied wall,*
*I pluck you out of the crannies.*
*I hold you here, root and all, in my hand."*

I looked around the room. Most of the girls stared transfixed; the boys looked down and shuffled their papers. Jenny shifted uncomfortably in her seat and put her head in her hands. In my mind I finished the poem along with Mr. Yeomans.

*"Little flower, but if I could understand*
*What you are, root and all, and all in all,*
*I should know what God and man is."*

He regarded the blossom for a moment, then released it and dusted pollen off his hands.

"Okay, your first homework assignment. Next class each of you bring me a flower. And extra credit for anyone who comes up with the author of that poem."

# CHAPTER EIGHTEEN

I DUCKED AS DAL'S LEFT CAME IN, CATCHING ME A GLANCING blow on the cheek. Our gloves were old and cracked, and a tab of stiff leather on the outer edge of his glove caught my skin and slit it like a knife. I wiped my face and saw a trace of blood on my glove; not enough to stop the fight. We had been sparring for five minutes and I was starting to get winded but I knew that Dal was, too.

He swung again and I blocked his glove with my left, slipped a right past his defenses and got him on the nose. He shook his head and stepped back while the crowd of kids laughed and yelled, then he got his gloves up again and came at me. I took a punch on the shoulder, blocked the other punches and made my way backwards around the mat.

I hadn't planned on any of this.

I had found out the first week of school just how much emphasis there was on sports. From the elementary grades on up, kids engaged in some kind of physical activity after school. All week long the teachers reminded us about tryouts on Friday and the coaches roamed around, armed with lists of student names. They stuck their heads inside the classrooms, they cornered kids in the halls, at lunch, on the playground, looking for the biggest or tallest and making them offers (or threats) of team involvement.

"Ever played football? Y' look to be capable; you're big enough."

"Need someone tall to play guard. How high can y' jump?"

"First year, right? Get over to the gym after last period. We'll figure sump'n out."

One of the coaches had tracked Jack down the very first day and tapped him for football, partially for his size and partially for the novelty of fielding a Yankee. I already knew I was too small for football, too short for basketball, and too slow for track because I'd tried all three, back in Shelton. The difference was that in Shelton you could satisfy the physical education requirement by just running around the gym for a half hour with a bunch of other kids. Here the coaches seemed determined to push everybody into some organized sport.

The gym was an older building perched on the far edge of the school grounds above the football field. Inside was a basketball court with bleachers on either side, showers and dressing rooms at one end, and the administrative offices at the other. This afternoon the basketball nets were pulled up and a group of boys were huddled in front of the bleachers. The coaches pushed them around, trying to form a line according to height. We took our places about midway along the row.

Over the next half-hour students were pulled out and sent off to various sports. Neither Dal nor I made the cut for football or basketball. One coach put us through a series of wind sprints that made it clear we weren't going to be track stars either. Finally, after some of the smaller, muscular boys were assigned to wrestling, the two of us were left standing with a group of about ten gangly kids.

At this point a couple of the older students rolled a thick mat out on the floor and the Head Coach brought out an old canvas bag. He looked us over as he walked the line, then he motioned me and Dal to step forward. He reached into the bag and brought out a couple of pairs of boxing gloves. He smiled as he tossed them to us.

"Last chance, ladies. Give us a good show or you're gonna end up in band."

"Shit, I hate this," Dal said under his breath as he pulled on his gloves

"Yeah, me too. Just don't hit too hard, okay?"

We walked out to the middle of the mat. I looked up and saw Jenny and Judge sitting toward the top of the bleachers. Down below students who had already finished their tryouts stood in a ring around us, yelling and chanting.

"Hey, Yankee, ya hit like a girl!"

"Dal, you're a pussy!"

We squared off. I tried a few half-hearted jabs and Dal did the same as we slowly walked around, trying not to either hit too hard or get hit. More and more kids gathered.

"C'mon, you're not even trying!"

"Hit 'im, Dal, hit 'im!"

The noise got louder and the kids pushed closer. Whenever Dal and I got too near the edge they would reach in and shove us back toward the center. Coach didn't try to stop them. After one shove I stumbled and grabbed Dal in a clinch to keep from falling down. We held onto each other for a minute, trying to catch our breath. By now each of us had landed a couple of good hits on the other, and despite my promise I was starting to get angry.

"Whaddaya, queer? Quit huggin' him!"

"C'mon, Dal, finish him off!"

"Fight, fight, nigger and white! C'mon Yankee, beat that white!"

I pushed Dal away and stepped back, keeping my gloves up. Both of us were panting and I was dripping with sweat. I thought about the situation. If I won I might get a lot of pressure to turn out for boxing and if I refused I'd be labeled as a sissy. It was bad enough being an outsider; I didn't want to be a target for the rest of the school year.

I shook my head to get the sweat out of my eyes, then lunged forward and knocked Dal's gloves aside with my left. I followed with strong right straight to the eye. He stumbled backwards and the kids stomped and yelled, turning on him.

"Awright, hit 'im again!"

"Dal's gettin' beat by a Yankee!"

Dal blinked and wiped a glove across his eye to clear it and I tapped him again, knocking his glove back into his nose. For the first time I saw a flash of anger cross his face. He lashed out with a wild left. I ducked under it, hit him on the side of the face, and straightened up. He cursed and came at me fast, and instead of blocking his punch I dropped my guard. He landed a perfect left hook on my nose, my feet flew out from under me, and I fell flat on my back, my head bouncing off the mat. There was an explosion of cheers for Dal, combined with yells for me to get up and fight. I stayed down and got my breath back, glad for a chance to rest.

Coach pushed his way through the crowd and yelled at me to get up, dammit, and stop bleeding on the mat. Dal helped me over to a seat on the bleachers; Coach looked briefly at my nose and split lip and handed me a wet rag.

"You ain't never gonna make it in the ring. Keep yer head down for a minute, then git outta here and go see the school nurse."

Dal left to get some water. As I sat alone on the bench, my head between my knees, someone sat down beside me and put a hand on my shoulder. A friendly voice said, "Here, let's check out the damage." I looked up to see Mr. Burroughs. He patted me on the shoulder, tilted my head back and gently wiped my nose and mouth with the rag.

"Good thing this isn't permanent. Ever played a musical instrument? We need another clarinet."

I was still stunned from the punch but I nodded. He took my chin in his hand once again and tilted my head upward, looking closely.

"You've got a good-looking mouth for the clarinet. Take care of it with some Vaseline and that split lip should heal okay. Come see me in a week or so." He gave me a final pat on the shoulder and turned away.

In the office the school nurse took one look at my lip and shook her head. She made it clear she wasn't a fan of the weeding-out process.

"I just don't know. Every year these coaches, they're lookin' for the biggest and the toughest. Every year someone ends up like you or worse. I swear I spend most of the first week of school patchin' kids up from this tryout nonsense or some stupid fight out there on the playground. Seems like everybody's gotta try to be the big dog..."

Her voice trailed off as she cleaned the cut on my lip. When she was done she bent my head back, looked up into each nostril with a light, and wiggled my nose from side to side. I let out a yelp and jerked my head away.

"That hurt? I'm not surprised. You're lucky it's not broke. Take this Kleenex and blow. Gently! Okay, now hold still." She swabbed away the worst of the blood and gave me some cotton to pack in my nose. "Who did this to you? Must have been a mean 'un. You don't want to be around kids like that." I looked sideways at Dal; he looked a little guilty and a little proud at the same time. The nurse finished cleaning me up, gave me some aspirin and a note to Dad and Mom, and warned me about future fights.

"I guess it's band for the two of us," I said as we walked home. "Mr. Burroughs told me to come see him once my lip gets better."

"Yeah, I'll be there, too. I started with the clarinet in junior band last year and I was figurin' to play again this year. And what about those scholarships—Band

Camp down in Miami next summer? He said I had a chance." He looked hopeful. "Maybe you and I'll both get to go. Wouldn't that be great? Did you know he's one of the Scoutmasters, too? I've been in Scouts for a year now and he and Mr. Yeomans…"

"Hey, wait a second." I thought back about what we'd just gone through. "What was all that about having to take band if we didn't get on some team? Now you're telling me you already planned to take band. Why didn't you just sign up? Why'd you end up having to box with me?"

"Shoot, everybody has to try out for something. It's kind of a ritual." He hesitated. "Remember there were only a few of us left and Coach asked who wanted to go first? I raised my hand and nodded at you and he picked you too. Look, there were some of those kids left for tryouts that're skinny like us; they wouldn't be in football or basketball, but you don't want to go up against them 'cause they're flat mean. Couple of 'm are Clayton's friends and I figured they were fixin' to kick hell out of you for what happened earlier. And if you put up a fight it would just make things worse, prob'ly for the rest of the year. So this way…" He looked at me and smiled. "Anyway, we're friends. I was kind of surprised when you started actually hitting me, though. I didn't think you knew anything about boxing."

"Yeah, I had a plan, too." I grinned and touched my lip. "I just didn't know you had such a good left."

## CHAPTER NINETEEN

SATURDAY MORNING. DAL AND I SAT ON HIS FRONT PORCH with some water and a couple of sandwiches and the weekend stretching out before us. Dal's house was small, like ours, but it was built of wood instead of brick and looked like it hadn't been painted in years. The yard was bare dirt and sandspurs and a few scrawny trees. On the east side of the house a garden of collards, tomatoes, potatoes, and pole beans struggled in the heat, their scorched leaves hanging limp. Dal complained that the dirt didn't hold water, that he had to soak it constantly just to keep things from drying up and dying. In the shadow of the porch Dal's skinny, tan-colored hound lay sprawled on his belly, his head on his paws, taking advantage of the cool sand.

"What's your dog's name?"

"Boy, I guess."

"What?"

"His name. I just call him Boy, like, 'Here, Boy.' Doesn't matter what I call him; he doesn't come anyhow."

Boy looked like every other stray I'd seen hanging around Yeomans. They all seemed to belong to one large family and they were everywhere, lying in small groups by the side of the road and wandering through the neighborhoods. Nobody seemed to own them, at least I never talked to anyone who did, and I never saw anybody feed them either. They never moved except when they absolutely needed to, like when someone shied a rock or a stick at them, and when they did move it was in slow motion. I had tried a couple of times to get close to one for a better look, but when I got to within about ten feet the dog would get up, stretch, and saunter off in the opposite direction.

Boy turned toward Dal and cocked one ear when he heard his name, but in the dense heat even that slight activity seemed to be too much effort; he laid his head back down and closed his eyes.

"So, do you hunt him? What's he good for?"

"Nothing much, I guess. He just kind of sticks around, goes where I go. He's never far." Dal reached out and gave Boy a couple of pats on the back. Boy thumped the ground once with his tail.

"Wish I still had my dog," I said.

All of us kids had protested when we had to leave Chub in Shelton. Dad gave all sorts of reasons: Chub was too old to travel, he'd be uncomfortable in the heat, they'd found a farm near Shelton where he could run free and play with the other animals. We were skeptical and we said so. Dad wouldn't change his mind, but he did promise to talk about getting another dog once we arrived in Georgia. So far he and Mom had avoided the discussion.

"So, how'd you find Boy? Did you buy him?"

Dal laughed. "Oh, hell no. You don't buy a dog. He just turned up one day. I started feeding him and he stuck around."

Boy reached his head up over his back, gnawed vigorously on his rear end and then, exhausted by the effort, slumped back down onto the sand.

I was pretty sure if I asked for a dog Mom would say no, given the size of our house, and Dad would probably go along with her. Still...

"So does he eat a lot? Where does he sleep?"

Dal hesitated for a moment, like it was the first time he'd thought about these issues.

"Let's see, food. He gets table scraps, mostly. Never seems too hungry. I think he chases stuff down like all the other dogs here. And he doesn't much like to come in the house. I'd say he's an outdoor dog, just a typical dog, y' know." He seemed ready to move on from this conversation. "So, we gonna go on out to the river?"

"You bet." I tied my camping gear on behind the bicycle seat and we wheeled out of the yard. When we were a block away I looked back to see Boy still lying flat on the sand. Apparently he had more sense than to exert himself in the midday sun.

So: free dog, finds his own food, stays outdoors. I thought about Mom and Dad's arguments against having a dog. Maybe I'd found an answer.

## CHAPTER TWENTY

Dal's favorite camping spot was on high ground across the road from the Yeomans' farm, about a quarter mile back from the river bank.

"This'll be a good dry run for the Scout trip," he said as we pedaled along slowly in the heat. "Jenny's family owns the property and she said her dad doesn't mind if we camp there. Kind of interesting, there's this little hill and everything else right around it is pretty flat. Jenny says it's an Indian mound and she's got pots and arrowheads and stuff from there she says her granddaddy dug up."

Biking out to Jenny's place took us almost an hour and by the time we pulled up to her gate we were both drenched with sweat. Down at the end of the driveway was a huge old farmhouse with a screened-in porch on three sides, the front yard a dense jungle of flowering plants and trees that almost blocked the place from view. We rode down the driveway to find Jenny standing on the porch, hands on her hips. She looked at us through the screen and shook her head.

"Y'all must be the dumbest things in creation, out in this heat. Where y'all headed?"

"Goin' up on the mound for an overnight," Dal replied.

"Got water? You sure don't want to drink from that river."

I showed her my canteen; Dal did the same. Jenny shook her head again.

"Not near enough. Y'all 'r gonna fry out there. Come on in and set for a while. I'll get you another jug to carry along." She disappeared into the house.

Dal and I sat down at a table near the front door, flanked by a stack of firewood on one side and an ancient chest style freezer on the other. After a minute Jenny reappeared with iced tea. She grinned at me. "Got some lemon in this; not sweet like the lunchroom stuff," she said. We sat and talked and waited for the day to cool off, and after a while she and Dal got into a discussion of some teachers and classes I didn't recognize. By now I'd had way too much tea and asked Jenny for the bathroom. "In through the kitchen, around the corner," she said, pointing vaguely. I left them and wandered inside.

Directly behind the porch was a huge kitchen, with a table and chairs and a wood-burning stove and several small couches over in a corner alcove. At the back of the kitchen a set of stairs led up to the second floor, and just past the stairs was a formal dining room filled with old, heavy furniture. Most of the surfaces were completely covered with books and papers and bones and shards of pottery. An alligator skeleton squatted at one end of the dining room table; at the other end stood a stuffed hawk, his talons gripping a small branch.

I continued through the house and found the bathroom tucked underneath the stairs in back. When I came out I turned to the right, and through a partly open door I could see windows on the other side of a room, leading out to the porch. I pushed the door wide. Outside Dal and Jenny were arguing about which English teacher was hardest, but for the moment my attention was on the room's huge fireplace, the mantelpiece, and the wall behind it. I had walked into a museum.

Two human skulls sat on the far end of the mantelpiece, surrounded by metal tools and scraps of bone. I moved closer. The scraps of bone were fashioned into hooks and blades and bound with rawhide. Among the tools were syringes, needles, a pair of pliers and a short, wicked-looking saw. The rest of the mantelpiece was crowded with grey, undecorated pots made of some sort of chalky clay, all in perfect condition. The walls were hung with swords and rifles, large framed paintings and letter-sized documents, and smaller frames containing pieces of paper money. One piece lay by itself on the mantel, and I walked over and picked it up for closer study. Arching across the top of the bill were the words "Confederate States of America," in the middle was a sailor seated on some bales of cotton, at one end was the number "5" engraved in an ornate circle, and at the other end two women stood, one of them holding an old-fashioned set of scales.

"That'd be about a century old, 1861."

The bill fluttered to the floor as I jumped and turned around. The door I had just come through had swung back, and behind it was Mr. Yeomans, sitting in a huge old leather recliner with a newspaper in his lap. He had a slight smile on his face and was obviously enjoying my discomfort. I felt like I had been caught stealing.

"Mr. Letour, isn't it?" I nodded. "When you pick up one of these you need to use tweezers. The oil on your fingers plays hell with the rag content."

He rose from his chair and came over to retrieve the money from the floor. "This one here isn't real valuable, too many of 'em made. Still, it's in excellent shape." He held it up to the light, then placed it back on the mantel. "I like to study 'em for the engraver's art. 'Cause, just like they say about land, they're not making any more of 'em. You interested in the Civil War?"

"No, sir," I replied, "I mean, I don't know anything about it. I'm not from here."

"Defining event of our state, at least everyone acts like it was. Probably a good idea to understand what it was all about. You might get some information in class, this being the Centennial celebration of Georgia leaving the Union and all. It'll help you know the basics, maybe explain the way some people act." He paused for a moment. "Lord knows, sometimes nothing else does."

I stood there, not knowing what to say. Mr. Yeomans smiled again.

"Jenny's mentioned you; nice to meet you more formally than as just another student. By the way, I got the impression you knew who wrote that poem?"

I nodded. "Alfred, Lord Tennyson, sir. It's one of my mom's favorites. She's been telling it to us kids as long as I can remember." Dal yelled from the porch that it was time to get going. Mr. Yeomans sat back down in his big leather chair and filled his pipe.

"We going to see you at the Scout's camping trip next week?" I said yes and he turned back to his newspaper, waving me out.

"Welcome to Georgia, son," I heard him call as I left. "Welcome to the South."

## CHAPTER TWENTY-ONE

I BROUGHT UP THE SUBJECT OF CHUB'S REPLACEMENT AT Sunday dinner. It was one of the few times in the week we were all together, a time when Mom and Dad were usually pretty relaxed, so I figured I'd slip the idea into the conversation.

"Absolutely not," said Mom immediately, putting her knife down hard on her plate. "We have little enough space in this house as it is and we certainly don't need another mouth to feed." She looked over at Dad, daring him to support my suggestion. Dad indicated that he had a mouthful and continued to chew in silence.

"He won't cost anything," I said. "Dal's dog doesn't. Dal said he just turned up one day and stayed."

"Oh, no, we're not having one of those strays around our house. Chances are they're infested with worms and who knows what kinds of diseases. The vet bills alone would cost an arm and a leg, not to mention the dog food."

"Mom, I'm making money mowing lawns. If I can find a dog that looks good I can have him checked over before we ever decide. And I can pay any vet bills if it comes to that. And we always have a few leftovers anyhow; he could eat them instead of us throwing them out. I know how much you hate to waste food."

By now Dad had put down his fork and was following the back and forth between me and Mom, his chin in his hand. I thought I saw the hint of a smile on his face.

"This won't be like Chub. I'll look for one of the short-haired dogs so he doesn't stink and he doesn't shed. I'll walk him and I'll take care of him and..."

"Will, we just don't have room for another living thing in this house, and that's that!"

I could tell she was ready for the debate to be over, and she was irritated that Dad hadn't yet said anything to back up her argument.

"That's just it, Mom, he doesn't have to live in the house. There's all sorts of wood scraps behind the cabinet shop. They just burn 'em for trash; I can make a doghouse out by the back steps and I promise he'll never come inside if you don't want him to."

Mom looked harried and a little trapped. "Well, I don't know." She turned to Dad, who still hadn't said anything. Usually the two of them put up a united front. We waited in silence for his answer.

"What about baby Mary? What about me?" Martha chimed in. We all looked at her in surprise. She hadn't said anything until now and suddenly she was on her feet with her hands on her hips and tears streaming down her face.

"You always told us the stories about how we learned to walk with Chub. How is baby Mary going to learn if we don't have a dog? And I need a dog, too, just as much as Will, 'cause of that kid at school. That Elwood Burris, the one that calls me a nigger lover and says he's going to stick me with his knife." As she talked she got more and more upset. "Sally DiAngelo said the kids used to call her a Catlicker and give her a hard time 'cause of church. But she got a dog, and he walks to school with her and he stays until she gets out and he walks her home and now the kids don't dare bother her..."

She stopped to take a breath and a tear dripped off her nose. Mom put her hands up, palms out, waving a truce.

"All right, all right, that's enough for now. We'll talk more about this later. I swear..."

She got up and stalked out of the kitchen.

After everyone was finished, Martha cleared the table and I stuck around to help. Elwood was one of Clayton's friends and I wanted to know more.

"Well, he did call me that name once and he showed me a little knife he had. But Becky was there too and she told him she'd kick him in the balls if he ever tried anything. She does have a dog, though; I see him around school sometimes." She smiled sweetly and scrubbed another plate.

I was suddenly seeing my little sister in an entirely new light.

## CHAPTER TWENTY-TWO

"WELL, SHIT."

It was early evening on my first camping trip with the local Boy Scout troop. We'd had just enough time to get the poles up under the heavy canvas and stake down the corners of the tent before the sky turned black and the rain struck. Dal was hunkered down in the back of the tent, pushing his pack and his clothes away from under the leaky roof.

"Hope this lets up pretty soon, else we're in for a long night. Good thing I brought some extra clothes." He curled his sleeping bag in a half-circle to avoid the water pooling in the middle of the tent floor. "So anyway," he continued, "Besides camping, we get to go swimming at Mr. Burroughs' houseboat. Sometimes Mr. Yeomans comes along and shows us animals and stuff. Last year..."

The trees outside became sudden silhouettes as

the lightning struck, and the rest of his words were drowned out by a crash of thunder. The rain increased. Judging by Dal's cursing in the back of the tent, so did the leak.

The downpour continued for a few more minutes, then shut off abruptly as if from a faucet. The sounds of the forest gradually returned, birds calling and other animals moving around in the undergrowth. One of these animals appeared out of the leaves and slithered across the clearing in front of the tent. It was a small and brightly colored snake, blunt at both ends, banded with stripes of yellow and black and red. I pinned it down with a stick to take a closer look. Dal was still occupied in the back of the tent, arranging himself and his gear to avoid the growing puddle.

"Hey, can you reach my pack?"

"Just a minute. Shit." More movement inside. "Okay, what?"

"Throw me my jacket; it's in the pack, right on top."

The jeans jacket landed beside me. I grabbed it and wrapped it around the snake.

"Back in a second. I'm gonna show this to Mr. Yeomans."

I kept a tight grip on my package as I walked to the other end of the campsite. The troop leaders had picked a sandy clearing on the banks of the Altamaha River for the camping area. The site had a couple of decrepit wooden shacks that we had been warned about—homes for snakes and spiders and the occasional possum. It also had a privy that no one wanted to use (again because of the animals) and enough room to pitch half a dozen two-man tents.

I found Mr. Yeomans instructing a couple of other scouts in the art of campfire cooking. The afternoon shadows had lengthened out into twilight and he had two Coleman lanterns burning to help illuminate the cooking site. He looked at me cradling my coat and raised an eyebrow.

"What's that you're holding so carefully, Mr. Letour?"

"A snake, sir. You said we should let you know if we saw any snakes we didn't recognize, and I sure don't know what this is."

There was sudden silence, and the two scouts moved away from me and over to the other side of the fire. Mr. Yeomans put down his cooking utensils. I had his full attention.

"This, uh, snake. Is it pretty secure inside that jacket, son?"

"Yes, sir. Well, I think so. Anyway, he hasn't moved much since I picked him up."

"You picked him up. Did he bite you?"

"No sir. I held him down with a branch and wrapped him up before he could."

Mr. Yeomans relaxed visibly. The scouts came in a little closer but gave themselves lots of room to move.

"Okay, just stand there for a second and we'll have a look at him."

He cleared a space on the collapsible camp table, then stepped into his tent and brought out a forked stick and a large glass collection jar with a perforated metal top. I laid the jacket on the table and Mr. Yeomans unwrapped it.

For a minute I thought the snake had somehow escaped, and then I saw his blunt head poking out of one of the sleeves. Mr. Yeomans pinned the snake close to its head with the stick, then picked it up behind the jaws with his thumb and forefinger, cradling its body with his other hand. He dropped it tail-first into the jar and quickly clapped on the screw-top.

"Sam, Ellis, go round up the rest of the campers and see if you can find Mr. Burroughs. It's a little early for dinner but a good time as any for a biology lesson. Mr. Letour, why don't you stick around here with me."

The other boys took off at a run. Mr. Yeomans looked at me, then at the snake writhing in the jar, then back at me again. He took a deep breath and started to speak, then closed his mouth and sighed. "Mr. Letour, when I said to be on the lookout for snakes I didn't mean for you to pick 'em up. What kind of snakes do you have out West? Anything even remotely poisonous?"

"No, sir." I could feel my face redden with embarrassment. "We have rattlers in Eastern Washington but where I live it's mostly just garter snakes. I was careful, though; it didn't bite me."

"Damn good thing, too. I'd hate to have to explain to your parents if it had."

By this time more campers were crowding around the table. Mr. Yeomans looked around the group and counted heads.

"Okay, we're missing someone. Dal. And where is Mr. Burroughs?"

"He went to the store for hot dogs, sir."

"No, he's just back," another camper said. "I saw him down to the other end. I think Dal's with him."

"Right here, Andrew." Mr. Burroughs stepped into the firelight with Dal in tow. Both were carrying heavy grocery sacks. "I just needed Dal to give me a hand carrying the dinner fixings."

Mr. Yeomans acknowledged him impatiently and then directed everyone's attention to the snake, which was coiled up quietly in the jar.

"All right, everyone. Mr. Letour has provided us with the subject for tonight's biology lesson. At some risk to himself, I might add. Does anyone know what we have here?"

I heard some muttering about colors and, "Well, I'm not sure, might be a king." "No, man, look at the bands. That thing'll flat kill you..."

Mr. Yeomans interrupted the chatter. "Gentlemen, this is a coral snake. It may be small and it may be slow, but its venom is as deadly as a cobra and it *can* kill you. Look at the stripes." The scouts leaned in carefully, still keeping a respectful distance. "The red is next to the yellow. That's the key. There's a scarlet king snake that looks similar, but he's not poisonous and he's pretty shy. You almost have to force him to bite you. Our coral snake here is a little more skittish and he won't hesitate to chomp you if you irritate him enough. Now, on the king, the red and black rings are next to each other. The coral snake always has red rings smack up against the yellow. So remember, with your king snake it's "Red on black; friend of Jack." "Red on yellow; kill a fellow" is the coral."

We all looked closely at the patterns. Suddenly the camping trip had become a little less carefree.

"I'm going to keep this guy safe from you all, and vice versa," said Mr. Yeomans. "Next time you see him it'll be in the biology trailer and we can talk some more about his lifestyle. Mr. Burroughs, would you please take charge and help these boys get dinner ready."

He picked up the jar and headed back toward his tent. As he passed by me on the way he stopped. "Mr. Letour, you didn't seem too concerned about our little friend here. I take it you're not afraid of snakes."

I thought for a minute. "No sir. I get along with most animals pretty well. Like I said, I've never been around anything poisonous so I didn't know to be afraid."

Mr. Yeomans nodded thoughtfully. "A word of advice, son, as you're new here. Be careful with the local flora and fauna until you do know what to expect."

## CHAPTER TWENTY-THREE

IT TOOK A WHILE TO GET USED TO BIOLOGY CLASS. MR. Yeomans didn't give us pop quizzes or papers like the other teachers. He said we'd only have two tests, a midterm and a final, and we'd get everything we'd need to pass. That was all we cared about. Also he didn't act like he knew absolutely everything. We could even disagree with him if we had a good argument. And then he had the habit of ending each class with poetry. Sometimes he'd look around like he expected one of us to know the poem and chime in. Sometimes he'd even catch my eye and raise an eyebrow, like he was asking, "Want to give this one a try?" I could have, I guess, but I was having enough trouble just getting through the day with the other students; I didn't need any more attention. He never read the poems; he'd just say them from memory like he was talking to us. Jenny always seemed a little embarrassed when he did it, but I think she was also kind of proud.

"Dad's says there's a lot more to the world than just this place and I should 'broaden my horizons,'" she would say. Then she'd always follow up with, "I can't wait to get the hell out of here."

Today's class was about Charles Darwin's trip on the ship *Beagle*, when he sailed down to the Galapagos Islands and figured out evolution. Mr. Yeomans explained how animals and plants adapt to their surroundings. He had brought in a large poster with drawings of birds and hung it on the plant wall.

"Look at these birds," he said, walking back and forth in front of the drawings and tapping on them to make his point. "They all have the same body style, with about the same size and shape and wings and tails. They're all obviously finches. Not hummingbirds, not owls, not chickens. Finches. But now look at their beaks." He pointed out that, between birds, the beaks were entirely different. He explained that some were long and thin, good for drilling into cactus and pulling out grubs; some were short and heavy and perfect for cracking seeds.

"These birds adapted to survive. When they first came to these islands they all looked pretty much the same..."

I usually paid attention, but I'd read the chapter on adaptation already and the day was warm and humid and Jenny was sitting in the desk next to me. I was distracted. Jenny never used perfume but she had her own nice smell and I always knew when she was nearby. She and Dal and I had taken over the seats nearest the door into the classroom, and furthest from Mr.

Yeomans' desk. Jenny said she sat there because she didn't want to call attention to herself by sitting near her Dad, I was there because I liked sitting next to her, and Dal just kind of naturally ended up wherever we were, to round out the group.

Jenny shifted in her seat and leaned against me for just a second. I closed my eyes and enjoyed the moment but I was too self-conscious to lean back toward her. I always felt kind of funny and nervous around her, which was strange because she wasn't my ideal of pretty. She was thin and wiry and tough, and she hadn't developed a chest like some of the girls. She was more interested in animals than boys and liked to drive her Dad's little tractor around the farm, putting out feed for the goats and making sure the chickens hadn't made a complete mess of the garden. She sneered at most of the girls her age, girls who dressed up and put on makeup and hung on their boyfriends' arms. I'd never seen her talk much with any of the boys except to give them a hard time, like she'd done with Clayton. As far as I knew she didn't have a boyfriend and, all in all, I think the boys were kind of frightened of her. They sure gave her a lot of space.

My daydreaming was interrupted when I heard Mr. Yeomans say the word "dog."

"Next week our class is going to focus on one of my favorite species: the dog. How many of y'all have a dog?" Almost all the boy's hands went up. "Anybody got an Old Yeller type hound, that basic swamp dog you see everywhere around here?"

Dal gave me a grin and put up his hand.

"All right, Dal Royce," said Mr. Yeomans. "Be much

obliged if you could bring your dog along next week. We'll discuss him and do a little analysis of the species."

He finished up the class with a poem by Browning:

"The year's in the spring, the day's in the morn; Morning's at seven, the hillside's dew-pearled..."

When he got to the last verse he said, "Okay, last chance. Anybody know the ending...? 'God's in his heaven'...?"

Jenny gave a little sigh of exasperation, her usual response to her Dad's poetry. I felt his eyes on me as I looked down at my book. This poem was another favorite of Mom's and I could recite the whole thing from memory, but I still wasn't ready to draw any attention to myself.

## CHAPTER TWENTY-FOUR

IT HAD BEEN ALMOST A MONTH SINCE BOXING TRYOUTS, AND Mr. Burroughs had given me a pass on starting band until my lip was healed. I'd sat in on the class to get some practice fingering notes on the clarinet and reading music, but I was getting a late start on the actual playing. My only experience with musical instruments had been the previous year in Shelton, where I had played recorder in junior band and fooled around with the clarinet whenever I had the chance. I was beginning to wonder if I would ever catch up with the rest of the class. I had taken the clarinet home every night for the last week and tried blowing a few notes, just hard enough to get a sound but not enough to split my lip again. Now I was ready to play.

"Everybody, listen up," said Mr. Burroughs, "I need your attention. That's everyone, *now*. Charles; put down the brushes, please. Charles!" This last was directed at one of the drummers, Charlie Echols, who was working on the cymbals, trying to synchronize the *"shhhhh ch ch shhhhh ch ch"* of the brushes with the metallic *"clap"* of the top hat. He had been working on this since the first day of band and hadn't succeeded yet. Mr. Burroughs would grit his teeth whenever something complicated turned up in the percussion sheet music, and Charlie's performance usually lived up to his worst expectations. Fortunately, we had a surplus of drummers and Mr. Burroughs kept his temper under control by limiting Charlie to cymbals and the triangle.

"Thank you. Finally!" He glared at the room. "Okay, so far we've been concentrating on the upcoming football season. We're going to continue to work on "Colonel Bogey" and the Sousa marches and our fight song, and we should have those all down pat before the first game." He had decided to have us stay up in the bleachers instead of going down on the field, saying that we were more likely to achieve perfection if we didn't have to worry about where our feet were going.

"There are two other things that are really important this year. One is Spring Regionals and the other is Miami Band Camp, right after school lets out in the summer. Let's talk about Band Camp first. I've got two student scholarships to give out this year. Each scholarship is an all-expenses paid week studying with the music department at the University of Miami. That's transportation, food, housing, everything."

The room was silent. He had our complete attention.

"Now, the biggest challenge for me will be making a decision about who to send. Some of you have been in band for years and you have a lot of experience, and some of you are brand new, so I can't judge you just on how well you play. There's only one fair way to pick who gets to go: see who makes the most progress between now and the end of the school year. And in order to keep it completely fair, I need to hear you each play something you've never played before. That's where Regional comes in."

He picked up a stack of sheet music from his desk and walked around the room, handing each of us our score. "This year there's a new competition category: 'Original Composition.' All bands get judged on the assigned music, as usual, but any band that plays an original piece gets extra credit. You remember that we came in second place last year?"

Dal shook his head and muttered, "Yeah, we got robbed."

"This year we're going to come in first," Mr. Burroughs went on, "and we're going to do it with this piece that I wrote over the summer. I call it 'Sunrise, Yeomans County'". He gave us a few minutes to look at our parts and then told us to put down our instruments.

"We're going to go over the music line by line in just a moment. Right now I want you all to get comfortable, close your eyes and just listen while I describe the sound I'm going after." When everyone was quiet he said, "Here's the setting. I have a houseboat out on the Altamaha. It's just a little place, right on a bend of the river, a quiet spot..."

He walked around the stage, pausing a little at each section of the band as he talked. No one made a sound.

"Sometimes in the summer I wake up early, just before sunrise. I take a cup of coffee out on the deck and sit in the darkness, listening to the birds and insects tuning up; getting ready for the day. So sit there with me now and watch as the sky starts to get red, and then yellow, and then gradually the underside of the clouds take on a pinkish glow..."

He kept talking as he came across the stage, through the strings and into the woodwind section where he paused, standing between me and Dal. I opened my eyes a little bit and squinted sideways. Dal had his eyes closed tight. Mr. Burroughs put his hand on my shoulder as he continued to describe the early morning.

"The trees over the river were black shadows before, but now you can begin to see individual branches. The sun touches the leaves and separates them from each other; with more and more light you can see the outline of the river as it passes the houseboat and straightens out, stretching like a big, golden highway toward the coast. And the colors gradually get stronger, more of the birds wake up and chime in, and you watch and you listen as they finally build up to a climax of sound just as the sun comes up right in the middle of the river."

I saw the scene perfectly, almost as if I were there, and it was a moment before I realized that Mr. Burroughs had stopped talking. I opened my eyes. There was silence as the other students blinked and shifted in their seats. I looked over at Dal. He looked slightly uncomfortable. I wondered if Mr. Burroughs had been rubbing his shoulder too.

"All right, everyone, let's get to work," Mr. Burroughs said. His words sounded almost harsh after the soothing picture he had painted. "We've got a lot to do."

## CHAPTER TWENTY-FIVE

SATURDAY MORNING. I KNELT IN DARKNESS INSIDE THE cramped confessional box, my face close to the screen that separated me from Father Donovan just a few feet away. The air inside the confessional was hot and damp and still. I could smell the perfume and sweat left there by the other parishioners who had come to Confession before me. Father had a wooden panel that he could slide across each of the screens to block out sound, but even through this panel I could hear the muffled voice of someone on the other side reciting his sins. I swatted away a mosquito and reviewed the past week, tallying up my numerous failures, while my knees complained at the lack of padding on the prie-dieu underneath me.

Father Donovan's voice rose in volume from a consoling murmur to an audible statement of absolution and finally the words, "Go in peace." He shut the panel on the other side of his booth and I knew he would sit for a moment in silence before opening mine. I tried to imagine what it must be like for him each week, listening to people pour out their shame in large and small doses. If they were like me they would be returning again and again with the same story. He probably needed a rest between sinners.

The wooden panel rattled open. In the gloom I could see the vague outline of Father's shoulders and his large, bald head. I knew he was wearing a robe and a stole and I felt sorry for him because I only had on a t-shirt and already I was soaked in this heat. He cleared his throat. I made the sign of the cross.

"Bless me, Father, for I have sinned. It's been one week since my last Confession. These are my sins. I fought with my brother two times, I took the Lord's name in vain three times, I teased my little sister..."

Back in Shelton sins like these had been the extent of my wickedness. Our parish priest, Father Andrus, was from Hungary and almost seventy years old; Dad said our little church was his last assignment before retirement. Father Andrus struggled with English and hardly ever talked to anybody outside of Sunday Mass. I imagined hearing my confession must have been really boring for him. He would always listen in silence, never asking for any details, and when I was done he would assign exactly the penance as the week before: "Five time Hail Mary."

Here in Georgia my temptations had changed. In Shelton everyone was covered in flannel most of the year, but here everyone seemed to wear as little as possible and I suddenly realized that girls had curves. I was painfully aware of girls' bodies and my own body, and everything around me made me think of sex. The trouble was, I didn't have the slightest idea of what was happening to me or what I was supposed to do with these new feelings and desires.

Jack and his friends used terms like 'getting to second base' and 'going all the way', and I had to bug him until he explained what that meant. As for me, I had never intentionally touched a girl's breast or any other part of her for that matter, although I certainly would have if I'd had the chance and the guts. But then I would have been like the dog that chased the car and finally caught it. What would I do next?

I finished my short list of minor sins and hesitated for a moment. Father Donovan waited patiently. It was always easier to start with the venial sins, like cursing and teasing Martha, and then work up to the ones I was most ashamed of. Nowadays those all had to do with sex.

"Um, I was impure in thought, maybe ten times, and I was impure in deed, um, I think two times..." I always reported a number that was lower than the truth. That in itself was a sin, the sin of lying, and to a priest, no less. But I was just too ashamed to say how much of my energy was directed toward sex.

"Were the impure deeds by yourself or with someone else?"

Oh crap. This was the same question he asked every week. I knew it was coming but I always hoped he would forget or spare me the embarrassment of admitting that I played with myself. It would have been so much more satisfying to say that I had a girlfriend and we had been making out and we had gone a little too far. Solitary jerking off seemed so unmanly, compared to having a real relationship...

All of my daydreams were about Jenny, of course, but I don't think she thought of me at all. If she did think about me I was pretty sure it wasn't as a boyfriend. We spent lots of time together but most of our activities included Dal, and having Dal along meant I never had a chance to say anything personal to her or even try to hold her hand. Mostly we were a threesome that talked about books and the places we wanted to go and what we wanted to do with our lives.

I realized that Father Donovan had asked me a question.

"Excuse me, Father?"

"By yourself or with someone else?" His voice sounded tired and a little impatient.

"By myself, Father."

"All right, then. Anything else?"

Of course. There was always something else. I hadn't even mentioned the wet dreams, when sometimes I would wake up after it was all over and sometimes I'd wake up in the middle and help things along. I knew it was a sin to actually touch myself, but was it a sin to have the dreams in the first place? Dad had never explained anything about sex, and I was too afraid to ask for fear he might think I was doing something sinful. Jack was no help either. God seemed to be giving him a free pass; he smoked and drank, bragged about the girls he'd gone out with, and didn't seem to care about any consequences. He seemed to have everything worked out for himself, but that didn't do me any good.

"Son, anything else?"

"No, Father."

"All right, then. Now, you realize that your body is a temple of Christ, and by each impure act you desecrate that temple. Every time...impure thoughts and deeds... weaken the foundation...increase the likelihood of further sin..." I half-listened to the warnings I had heard before, but it was all just words, and none of it seemed to help. And now I was afraid I was still in the state of sin because I hadn't admitted to having wet dreams.

"For your penance say three decades of the rosary and offer them up to our Holy Mother Mary." Through the screen I could see him make the sign of the cross as he finished with, "And now I forgive you your sins in the name of the Father, the Son, and the Holy Ghost. Go in peace."

He closed the panel. I stood up, left the confessional, and knelt down at one of the pews in the back to do my penance, feeling anything but peaceful.

# WINTER

## CHAPTER TWENTY-SIX

WE MADE IT THROUGH CHRISTMAS, BUT THERE WERE TIMES I thought we wouldn't because Christmas was so different here.

To begin with, there was no snow. We were expecting that; sometimes we didn't have snow in Shelton, either, but at least we had bitter cold and stinging rain that made staying indoors a treat. This year, Christmas day was 75 degrees and sunny. We kept the windows open to catch the breeze and suffered with the mosquitos that still got in the house in spite of the screens.

Then there was the tree. Each year for as long as I could remember we'd drive out into the country and spent the afternoon walking around in the snow and selecting our perfect tree. Then we'd all hold hands around it and sing the "Oh, Christmas Tree" song before we cut it down. This year we had just two choices: paying way too much for a tree that had been trucked in from Washington and was much the worse for the trip, or cutting down one of the scraggly local pines. We decided on a pine tree and hung about half the ornaments we were used to.

We also missed our usual holiday treats: fat red pomegranates, rock candy, tiny tangerines that made my mouth water just to look at them. Winn Dixie carried only the tangerines, so Dad brought one bag home and we all divided it up over Christmas week. Jenny had a pomegranate bush at her house but it was ornamental and the fruits were small and brown and bitter. And no one here had ever heard of rock candy.

One plus was the availability of mistletoe. Jack and I went out into the swamp a few blocks away, where the stuff grew wild up in the oak trees, and came back with a whole bushel basket full. Back in Shelton it cost half a buck for a small bunch; here we gathered enough in twenty minutes to decorate the entire house.

But the biggest thing missing this Christmas, at least for Mom, was the family church routine. Since we were a mission parish, a lot of the usual church services were either cut short or missing altogether. We hadn't gotten close to many people, even the other Catholics, so Mom had to deal with the absence of friends and family during the holiday season. The final straw for her, though, was Midnight Mass. Dad was junior to almost everyone else on the management team at the mill and he had to fill in when people took vacation time off. This meant that, for the very first time, Dad couldn't come to Midnight Mass with the family.

It was a couple nights before Christmas. Martha was asleep and Jack and I had just gone to bed. Dad had gotten home late again and was having dinner in the kitchen while Mom finished up the dishes. I heard them talking, quietly at first, then gradually Mom's voice got louder and louder.

"Tom, you promised!"

"Now, dear," Dad was using his reasonable tone again, "I don't have any control over the scheduling. We're working three shifts and we're not closing down Christmas Day, so somebody has to be there. You know I'd never miss Mass if there was any way, but I don't have any seniority now..."

There was the clatter of dishes in the sink and then silence. I could almost see Mom catching her breath, pursing her lips.

"GodDAMMIT!"

The outburst was so angry and so loud that for a moment I didn't believe it was Mom. Jack and I looked at each other, stunned. We crowded onto the corner of the hide-a-bed near the doorway of the TV room and listened.

"Now, dear..." I could imagine the shock and pain on Dad's face and I could picture him reaching out to her.

"No, don't, Tom. Just don't." Mom's voice sounded anguished and exhausted. I heard a chair scraping on the kitchen floor, quick steps clattering down the hall, and the slam of their bedroom door. Baby Mary started to wail almost immediately. She kept it up for a long time and it didn't sound like Mom was even trying to comfort her. A minute later another chair scraped across the kitchen floor and I heard Dad walk back to their bedroom.

Dad said something I couldn't hear. They started out quiet, then they went back and forth, louder and louder until finally Dad yelled, "Christ, Anne, what do you want me to do?" I uncurled myself and sat up and looked at Jack. He just shook his head and moved over to his side of the hide-a-bed without saying a word.

I turned off the light and lay there in the darkness. This was the first time I'd ever seen Dad faced with an impossible situation. He couldn't be two places at once; he couldn't go to work and at the same time make Mom happy by being with her in church.

I was beginning to think that Dad had gotten the short end of the stick and Mom was being unreasonable. But I knew she couldn't be unreasonable because Dad and Mom didn't argue. Mom said so; she used herself and Dad as examples when she took us kids to task for fighting with each other. More than once she had said, "Children, you don't hear your father and me fight, do you?" I had heard them discussing things and having differences of opinion, like whether to have another dog or not, but I'd never heard them yell at each other. This was totally contrary to the world as I knew it.

"Jack?"

"What? C'mon, I'm tired!"

"Have you ever heard them fight before?"

There was silence, then Jack rolled over and stood up beside the bed. He went to the dresser, pulled out a pack of cigarettes and crossed over to the window. There was usually a breeze through the house at night, and Jack had found he could blow cigarette smoke out the TV room window without any of the smell coming back into the room. He lit up and took a deep drag before answering.

"Nope. That was definitely a first. I know Mom really hates being here, but it's no picnic for Dad either. I figure there's nothing we can do about it, you and me;

it's between them." He took another drag and leaned way out in the yard to exhale.

"Well, what do you think about being here?"

"Oh, shit, I don't know." He smoked for a minute in silence. "Dad's never home, and Mom's always too busy with Mary and the house to pay any attention to me. I pretty much stay out of the way. I like cruising with Judge and the guys. Judge knows a guy who moonshines and sometimes we get that old Negro out on Shakerag Road to buy us some beer. I guess it's okay, but I sure don't want to live down here forever. Mom's been on Dad to move; I heard them the other night when I got up to pee."

"Anybody call you a Yankee? A nigger lover?"

He took one last drag and ground out the cigarette on the brick siding before he pulled down the screen and got back into bed.

"Naw. When we first got here a couple guys said something about Yankee this and Yankee that, but it's pretty much a joke anymore, especially since I play football. Nobody calls *me* a nigger lover." He punched his pillow a couple times. "I don't get this whole Civil War thing anyhow. That was all over a hundred years ago. I mean, we don't go to school with Negroes, we hardly ever even see 'em. If people have a problem with 'em down here it's nothing to do with me. I just try to fit in and hope we get the hell out of here soon."

He rolled over and in a couple of minutes he was asleep. I lay in the dark, trying to make some sense out of things and not getting anywhere.

## CHAPTER TWENTY-SEVEN

MISS MACDONALD FINISHED TAKING THE ROLL AND whacked the desk once with her steel-edged ruler. The room fell silent.

"Y'all know what day this is, don't you? Yes, I *know* it's Thursday, Cobb. Anybody else? No? Well, it's also January nineteenth. Georgia seceded from the Union one hundred years ago today."

There were muted rebel yells and whispers of "Damn Yankees!" Miss MacDonald picked up the ruler again.

"Settle down, everyone. This week we're going to study about the causes of the war, how each side reacted, and how it affected our state in particular. Georgia played a big role in the fight, and some even say the war ended here, when President Jeff Davis was captured just over in Irwin County. And Lord knows we had our share of suffering, especially when Sherman came through on his March to the Sea."

She came around and stood at the front of her desk. "I know there are strong feelings about the war. All of you've grown up with it, heard your families talk about it. Some of your ancestors fought and died in it. It's not an easy thing to study. There are some uncomfortable facts we have to talk about so you can understand how we got to where we are. And even though the war itself was a century ago, right now there are some things happening in the country – sit-ins in North Carolina, school integration – and they're going to affect you all sooner or later. So when your parents and your friends and relatives talk about events in the news, I want you to know what's behind them."

As she talked the class grew silent and tense. I felt as if all the other student's eyes were on me, but when I looked up everybody turned away to avoid my gaze. All except for Clayton. He looked straight at me, his eyes hard, shielding his mouth with his hand so Miss MacDonald couldn't see him mouthing 'Yankee' and 'Nigger lover.'

"Any of y'all tell me why the War happened? What have you heard?"

A forest of hands appeared, all of them except one belonging to the boys. Miss MacDonald called on each of the students and wrote their comments on the blackboard:

"The North tried to take away our slaves."

"The Yankees attacked us first."

"Lincoln was elected President."

"The Yankees tried to turn the Negroes against their owners."

"The Yankees tried to take away our freedoms."

She finally called on the one girl who had raised

her hand. The girl's name was Louise Bledsoe, and she was small and pretty and her curled blonde hair always had a ribbon in it. She was the kind of girl that Jenny would scoff at for being, as she put it, a 'Miss Priss', but Louise was determined to be heard. She held her hand up patiently, waiting for the boys to finish. When it was her turn she stood up and took a deep breath.

"Miss MacDonald, my mama says them Yankee soldiers were men of low moral character and they killed women and children and they stole livestock and mostly they didn't have no more soul than some animal." She finished in a rush and sat down, her face red with embarrassment from speaking up for the first time in class.

Whispers of agreement went around the room as Miss MacDonald wrote the basics of Louise's statement on the board. Then she laid down the chalk and walked back to her desk.

"Okay, a lot of what y'all said there is true, except for the North attacking us first, which isn't, but we'll get back to that later. What I wanted to get at was the fundamental reason for the War. Some people say it was economics, and that's partially right, but the main reason was slavery, pure and simple. Back in the 1800s cotton was the primary export from the south, even bigger than tobacco. The southern states supplied seventy-five percent of the world's cotton, and it was Negro slaves that made this possible. Some people say it was the North interfering with our way of life. We had slaves and they didn't. We didn't want them telling us to give them up. The question is: Why did we have slaves in the first place?"

She spent the rest of the hour talking about the

origins of slavery, how the Constitution recognized a Negro as only three-fifths of a person, and how the state Slave Codes defined a slave as 'a human being that has no freedom but is the property of another.' After a while some of the students lost interest and started poking at each other and fidgeting, but I hung on every word. Dad and Mom had never talked much about the Civil War, even when they told us we were coming to live here. I remembered reading about the War in my history class in Shelton, but it was just something we had to memorize along with the others, with names and dates like 1066 and the War of 1812; it sure had nothing to do with me. Now I realized that everyone in class took slavery for granted and had a grudge against the North because the war took their slaves from them. No wonder I was having a hard time fitting in.

When the lunch bell finally rang the rest of the kids gathered their things and headed for the door, but Miss MacDonald caught my eye and motioned me over.

"Was that your first encounter with the War, Mr. Letour? You seemed surprised when I explained what it was all about."

"Yes, ma'am." I couldn't think of anything else to say.

"I guess we all take the past for granted here," she continued. "Most everyone has a set way of remembering things, depending on the stories they've heard. I know the War happened a hundred years ago, but for some, like Clayton, it's just yesterday because his family lived it. Everybody here lived it. And he's probably not going to change how he feels about the South and the North and you. He's got no reason to change, and even if he had other information that wouldn't be reason enough." She sighed. "I don't know what else to say."

I thought about our conversation as I crossed the schoolyard, and by the time I came through the cafeteria doors I was furious. I pushed between a couple of students who were standing between me and the food line and suddenly came face to face with Louise Bledsoe, who quickly backed out of my way. For a moment I wondered why she had a startled look on her face; then I realized I must have looked as mad as I felt. I almost apologized but I remembered the way she had described the Union soldiers; the disdain and disgust in her voice, and I shoved past her without a word.

Dal was sitting at our table in the corner. Except for the times when Jenny joined us we were the only ones to sit there and sometimes that isolation bothered me, but today I was happy just to be left alone. I grabbed my tray from the food line just as the five-minute bell rang for the next period, threaded my way between the tables, and sat down across from Dal. I wasn't very hungry, and the fact that today was macaroni and cheese and lime Jello didn't help. Dal's appetite didn't seem to be affected.

"What was that about, Miss MacDonald after class?" he asked between bites. I poked at my food and didn't say anything for a minute, but the more I thought about my situation the angrier I got.

"Did you hear what she said about the War, and how slavery's part of the Constitution, and about how Negroes aren't a full person? Did you know all that stuff before? Jesus, nobody ever told me any of this.

My parents never said anything, but they must have known. Do you believe everything she said?"

Dal put down his fork and started to speak, then he looked past my shoulder and his eyes narrowed. Someone was standing directly behind me and without turning around I knew it was Clayton. I tried to push my chair back and stand up but his hands were on my shoulders, holding me in place. Cobb sidled over behind Dal and held him down, too.

"Git it now, Yankee?" Clayton clamped down hard on my shoulder and leaned over me, pushing me into the edge of the table. "What y'all did to our state, Louise Bledsoe was right. You ain't no more than some kind of animal. And my daddy says now the govmint wants us to go to school with niggers." He leaned harder. The table cut into my chest and made it hard to breathe. I tried to push back but my shoes slipped on the well-waxed floor.

The cafeteria had almost emptied out. Mr. Burroughs came through the side door looking around for his missing band students. Clayton saw him and his voice got lower and meaner.

"You know what kinda animal y'are? A pussy! You and him 're in band 'cause you cain't fight, and band is for pussies and queers." He bent down and put his full weight on my shoulders, hard enough to double me over the table. With his back to Mr. Burroughs he spat into the middle of my plate, then he leaned around and smiled at me. "I'll be comin' for you, Yankee." He and Cobb walked away.

Mr. Burroughs stopped at the table and raised an eyebrow.

"Everything okay, boys?" Dal and I looked at each other. "Well, then, finish things up and let's get to work, shall we? We've got a long way to go before we can compete at Regionals."

## CHAPTER TWENTY-EIGHT

IN THE NEXT CLASS ON CIVIL WAR HISTORY, MISS MAC-Donald talked about the Union Army's march across Georgia and major battles around the state, most of which were lost by the Confederate troops. A couple of students told stories that they said had been passed down by their parents—stories of homes burned, property destroyed, relatives killed in action and whole families being forced to forage in the woods for food because the Yankees had slaughtered their livestock and burned their crops.

Right before class ended she asked if anyone had a question. Elwood Burris raised his hand.

"Miss MacDonald, my Daddy said there's some a' them Nigras tryin' ta eat at a white restaurant in Atlanta. Is that true? He said they been comin' from up North, from Washington," – he glared at me – "sittin' down and not movin' 'til someone serves 'em. He said my uncle in Atlanta saw it in the paper. He says pretty soon the gov'm't is gonna make us go to school with Nigras." His voice rose. "They can't do that, can they? Nobody's gonna make me go to school with Nigras! And he said they're gonna outlaw the Klan, too!"

By this time the class was in an uproar. Kids were talking excitedly, some tried to yell questions at Miss MacDonald but their voices were drowned out by the general noise. A couple of rows away I saw Elwood and Clayton with their heads together. Clayton caught me looking at him and smirked.

"Quiet down, everyone, quiet down," Miss Mac-Donald called, whacking her desk with the ruler. She tried to answer Elwood but the lunch bell rang and the students were on their feet and heading out the door. Dal and I hung back for a minute.

"Jesus," I said, "If they didn't have enough reasons to hate me before, they sure do now." This was the first I'd heard about the sit-ins. Nothing like this had ever happened in Shelton.

"Y' know, I just took this for granted, I guess." Dal gathered up his books. "Negroes, they aren't the same as us. They got their own schools and bathrooms and places to eat. And the Klan, they always ride in the parade on the Fourth; have for years, and they carry the battle flag and folks yell for 'em. I just never knew anybody was bothered by it, but then I never knew anybody that wasn't from around here, either."

The next day Miss MacDonald switched from Civil War history to current events, which didn't help since the big news in the paper was about sit-ins up North. The class mood was angry and ugly, and as soon as the lunch bell rang Dal and I got out of the room fast, pushing our way through the crowd of students heading for the exit. Halfway down the hall there was a break in the row of lockers, a shallow alcove with the door to the janitor's closet. As we passed by the alcove somebody reached out and grabbed me and spun me around. I went down hard on one knee and fell against a locker. Then Clayton had me by the collar, up against the janitor's door, while two of his friends held onto my arms. He jammed his forearm up against my throat, cutting into my windpipe so I couldn't yell. Dal tried to push between us, but someone shoved him to one side and he fell down into a crowd of students. There were shouts of "Fight! Fight!"

Clayton ripped open my shirt with one hand; with the other he jammed something cold up against my chest. I twisted away from his forearm and looked down. It was a jar of Gerber's Baby Food with something yellow and brown inside. Mashed bananas; that's one of baby Mary's favorites, I thought automatically, and the next moment I felt a white-hot needle in my chest. I tried to turn away from the stink of Clayton's breath, but his arm was still pushed up under my chin. As I struggled I could hear Martha's voice in the back of my mind, heard her fear of being threatened and unprotected, and suddenly I couldn't stand the thought that things were going to be like this forever.

I jerked my head to the side, took a deep breath, and screamed in Clayton's face. He pulled back, startled, and the other kids loosened their grip. I shook my arms free, grabbed the front of Clayton's shirt, leaned back into the wall for support and kicked him

141

as hard as I could between the legs. He doubled over and lost his grip on the jar; it dropped to the floor, bounced once, and shattered. A yellow and brown scorpion emerged from the broken glass and scuttled for freedom. Screaming girls rushed to get out of its way while the boys cheered and tried to stomp it to death.

There was a burst of activity a short distance down the hall. Clayton's friends left him on the floor and moved back into the crowd just as Mr. Yeomans pushed through the ring of students and took in the scene. I stood bent over, my shirt completely torn down the front, while Clayton writhed on the floor. Mr. Yeomans stepped over Clayton and pulled my hands away so he could get a look at my chest. The sting was beginning to throb and swell, and I felt lightheaded.

"What's going on here?" He looked at me and then down at Clayton, who was curled up against the wall with his arms wrapped around his stomach, wheezing raggedly. "Someone said there was a scorpion?" Most of the remaining students said nothing; a few mumbled 'Yessir.'

"What kind was it? What color?"

"It looked mostly yellow, Mr. Yeomans."

"Maybe some brown stripes too."

"Prob'ly just one a them Little Devil scorpions, sir. Warn't more 'n a couple inches or so."

Mr. Yeomans shook his head and asked me if I felt well enough to walk to the nurse's office. I said I did; he pulled me to my feet and helped me down the hall. When I looked back Clayton had pushed himself into a sitting position up against the lockers. Judge had arrived and he was bending over with his face up close to Clayton's, Dal was talking to one of the boys who had held me, and Jenny stood to one side with her arms crossed, a disgusted look on her face.

By the time we got to the nurse's office I was dizzy and shaking. I sat down on the edge of the cot in the corner and caught my breath while Mr. Yeomans explained about the scorpion. While he was talking the nurse looked at the sting, took my pulse, checked my eyes and peered down my throat.

"Your vision blurry? Throat feel swollen? How about your tongue? You allergic to bee stings?" I answered no to everything.

"Sounds okay so far," she said when she was done. "You just lay down here for a minute, son." She turned to Mr. Yeomans and said, "His pulse is a little fast but that should come down pretty quick if he just stays put. I'll get some calamine lotion to put on it; we'll let him rest back here for a while. Maybe you could go by the cafeteria, grab a little ice for the swelling..." They left the room and as their voices trailed off I heard references to Clayton.

I lay back on the cot and closed my eyes. It had only been about ten minutes since Clayton first grabbed me but I felt as if the whole afternoon had passed by. I closed my eyes and played back the scenes like a midday matinee, feeling Clayton's arm up against my throat, his rotten breath in my face, the stabbing pain in my chest. I dozed off thinking about Jenny.

I woke up with a start when the nurse slapped a cold pack on my chest. Dal was sitting in a chair across the office. He smiled and waved; I waved back and closed my eyes again. After a few minutes the nurse shifted the ice to one side to check the sting.

"You're gonna have that swelling for a while," she said. "Keep that ice pack with you. I'm sending you home with some antihistamine tablets and some Calamine and a note to your parents. They may want to talk to the Principal about this." She handed me a folded piece of paper. "Dal, you live over that way. Maybe you can go with him?"

Dal gave me a hand up. Halfway down the hall I unfolded the note, read it, and threw it in the trash. I didn't need any more reasons for Clayton and his gang to pay attention to me.

# CHAPTER TWENTY-NINE

"DAMMIT! THIS ISN'T WORKING."

Dal and I were halfway across the park on our way back to school and Boy was in tow, tied to the back of Dal's bike. The dog had found a trail of red ants beside the path and sat down abruptly to investigate, pulling back on the rope hard enough that Dal lost his balance. I got off my bike and waited, wondering how long it would take to get to school if Boy kept this up.

Mr. Yeomans had asked Dal to bring Boy for his class on the origins of dogs, but neither of us knew what he had planned once he had him in the classroom. Dal was a little embarrassed at Boy's lack of dog skills and for the last week he had tried to teach him to at least come when called. So far he wasn't having any success. I personally questioned the wisdom of trying to teach Boy anything; Dal said I should shut up and give him a chance.

Dal looked at the dog with an expression of disgust. Boy had stretched the rope out as far as it would go in order to reach some shade, and now he was lying down in the dust under an azalea, looking hot and bored. Dal reached into his bag and offered a piece of leftover chicken from lunch, but Boy just sniffed it once, put his head on his paws, and closed his eyes.

"Well, hell," said Dal, "no more being nice here. We gotta go or be late for class." He strapped his lunch bag back on the frame behind his seat, pulled up the kickstand, and pedaled off, yanking Boy to his feet. The dog wore a look of pained resignation as he trotted along behind the bike, moving just slow enough to stretch the rope taut and just fast enough to avoid being either dragged or strangled. We rode through the dry, hot park to school, and Dal tied Boy to a tree behind Mr. Yeomans' trailer until it was time for biology class.

Mr. Yeomans took roll and moved us all outside, where we gathered in a circle to look at Boy. Mr. Yeomans asked Dal to call his dog's name. Dal did, and Boy raised his head briefly to look at us, then closed his eyes, stretched, and flopped his head down on the dirt once again. There was a moment of silence.

"That," said Mr. Yeomans, "is a perfect example of the preferred activity level of a Carolina Swamp Dog. Thank you, Boy, for sharing with us." The look on Dal's face told me he was relieved that Boy didn't have to perform, but he wasn't sure if Mr. Yeomans hadn't just made fun of his dog. It was something I knew you don't do in the South.

"Tell us a little about your dog, Dal."

Dal explained that Boy, older than a puppy but not yet full grown, had just shown up one day by the water tower. Dal started feeding him. Boy stuck around for the food but didn't interact with Dal much, and he tended to ignore people except when they were threatening him or holding something to eat. He wouldn't fetch, he wouldn't come when called, and he sometimes disappeared for days at a time. Dal had seen him all over town, sometimes alone, sometimes sauntering along with a pack, and once out by the river where Boy ambushed and killed a water snake.

When he was done talking he sat down and scratched Boy's ears. Boy's response was to open one eye and thump his tail, then close the eye again. Mr. Yeomans took over.

"Any of the rest of you have a dog that looks like Boy?" Several of the boys raised their hands. "Do they act the same way?" The students nodded, one of them saying with pride that his dog had even less energy than Boy. This started an argument about whose dog was lazier. Mr. Yeomans let the discussion go on for a minute and then stepped in.

"Thank you, everyone. You might be surprised to know that Boy, and all the others you see like him around here, are unique. Any of you heard of Dingoes? They're wild dogs from Australia, like Jindo's are native dogs in Korea. But here's what's interesting: They all look just like Boy even though they're from thousands of miles away. Nobody's sure, but some scientists think Boy's ancestors might have come to America when there was still a land bridge across the Bering Strait." Most of the class looked blank. Mr. Yeomans said he'd explain more about the geography later.

"I know this professor over at the University of Georgia in Savannah. A while back he started studying the wild dogs that run in packs over in the coastal swamps; said he was surprised how much they all look and act alike. The ones you see around town here, they're mostly brown and thin and pointy nosed, they're all short-haired, their tails are long with a fish hook curve up over their backs, they don't move any faster than they have to, and for the most part they stay away from people unless they're hungry. My friend's convinced that these dogs—he calls them Carolina Dogs—are a breed all by themselves. And he thinks that they look like Dingoes and other primitive dogs because they're so far down the evolutionary chain. He thinks they are what you might call your Basic Dog. Boy here is a perfect example."

At the sound of his name Boy opened one eye slightly and yawned. The students looked at him with new-found respect.

"I don't have any good pictures of Dingoes so we can't compare one of them with Boy, but I do have something that's even better," said Mr. Yeomans. "Wait here a second and keep studying this specimen." He went to his pickup, opened the door and brought over another slim, brown, pointy-nosed dog that looked a lot like Boy.

"Everybody, I want you to meet...well, we don't have a name for her yet; just got her last week."

He unleashed the new dog. She stood quietly for a moment, taking us all in, then she walked straight to Jenny's side and lay down, front legs parallel, back straight, head erect. She looked like some kind of royalty. Everybody stood silent while Jenny petted her and scratched her ears. Boy heaved himself up to a sitting position and gnawed at a flea, keeping a wary eye on this new arrival.

"Anybody know who we have here?" asked Mr. Yeomans. We all shook our heads. "This is one of the most primitive dogs in the world. She's a Basenji; well, part Basenji, actually. Her mama was a pure-bred and her daddy was a Carolina Dog—probably looked exactly like Boy here. So, a couple things to know about Basenjis. They're called the barkless dog of Africa, don't hardly ever bark but they will give a howl or a yodel if they're really upset. They're clean—they groom themselves like cats and don't have much of a dog odor. The purebreds tend to be a little high-strung, but she's going to have some lazy blood from her Carolina daddy so she ought to be a lot less touchy. That should make her good with kids. Now notice her tail, totally curled, whereas Boy's..."

As he spoke I remembered why she looked familiar. Dad had a subscription to National Geographic, and all the back issues had been on the living room bookshelf in Shelton. One of last year's magazines had a big article about King Tut and what treasure hunters had found inside his tomb when it was first opened. There were thrones and boxes and wooden chariots all jumbled up in a pile, and there was also a carved ebony statue of a god-dog called Anubis. The statue had been in exactly the same pose as this dog, totally relaxed and completely alert at the same time.

"...but we won't be able to keep her," Mr. Yeomans was saying. "I've already got an old coon hound, and he likes his privacy even more than he likes food, so there'd be sure to be a fight. I haven't hunted him in a long time and he might think he's being replaced. Wouldn't be fair to the old guy."

He finished up the class with more information about evolution and why he thought Boy and this new dog were related, but I wasn't paying much attention. I had only one thing on my mind. Here, I thought, is a dog Mom could learn to love.

After class I sat outside with the dog and petted her while Jenny helped her dad tidy the biology trailer and lock up for the weekend. When she'd finished she came out and dropped down on the ground beside us.

"You sure you don't want her?" I couldn't believe she'd be willing to let this beautiful animal go.

"Naw, we got old Major and he's more than enough for both me and Dad. He's still good for a few more years. Besides, he lets us know whenever there's anything moving around the property that shouldn't be there. This one doesn't bark a bit." She reached over and scratched the dog between the ears; the dog lowered her head and closed her eyes. "Real problem is, though, Major hasn't stopped howling since we brought her home, so it's hard on everyone. He gets hoarse and this one gets the shakes, and the noise is like to drive us all crazy."

The dog continued to lie at attention. I reached in and ran my hand over the short coat. The dog looked at me, then turned her head and licked my hand briefly.

Mr. Yeomans came by with a stack of books and papers, heading for the truck. He knelt down by the dog and stroked her flank.

"How did you get her?" I asked.

"One of the managers at the mill," he said. "Guy came over from Tennessee to help install some new bleaching equipment. Had a year's placement so he brought his family and the family dog, that prize purebred Basenji bitch I talked about. Well, one day she got out, or some stray got in, and this girl here is the result. She's pretty enough but just not perfect, according to him. Told the vet to put her down." Mr. Yeomans smiled grimly. "Vet's a friend of mine; he couldn't do it and called me. Now we need to find her a home." He looked at me. "Jenny said you don't have a dog. You interested?"

"Oh, you bet!" I got his promise not to give her away to anyone else, at least for a day or so, and took off for home.

## CHAPTER THIRTY

SATURDAY MORNING I WASHED THE CAR WITHOUT BEING asked and offered to take care of Mary, just for good measure. After lunch I cornered Dad and Mom in the kitchen and told them about Mr. Yeomans' offer. Mom's immediate reaction was just what I had expected, but when I described the dog's size and temperament and how clean she kept herself, Mom reluctantly said she was at least willing to take a look. Dad didn't say much, just that he knew the mill manager in question and wasn't surprised that he'd try to get rid of the dog.

After Sunday Mass Jack and Judge took off to scout the Hazelhurst stadium for next week's game. The rest of us drove out to the Yeomans place. When we got there Jenny was sitting on the porch with the dog beside her. From off in back of the house came the sad "Aroooooooohh!" of Old Major. I introduced Dad and Mom and Martha to Jenny. She offered us chairs, said her Dad would be right back, and went in the kitchen to bring out some iced tea. Then we all sat around for a while, making small talk. Jenny admired baby Mary, Mom kept a wary eye on the dog, and in the back yard Old Major continued his sad cries.

"Sorry about all the noise," Jenny said. "He's been that way ever since this little girl here arrived a couple weeks ago. Just doesn't like any other dogs around the place." Mom flinched a little at every howl and Jenny caught the pained look on her face. "Dad's got him tied up back by the snake shed right now. I could go take him further out in the woods if he's makin' too much of a racket."

"No, no, that's all right," said Mom. "It's just that he sounds so mournful. Is he in pain?"

Jenny laughed. "Naw, that's just the way they all sound. Whyn't y'all come out in back and meet him; you could see Dad working on the snakes, too, if you're interested."

Mom stiffened. As long as I could remember she'd been afraid of all cold-blooded animals, including the little garter snakes and frogs that used to show up in our yard after the spring rains. Poisonous snakes were number one on the list of things she feared about living in the south. She wasn't all that comfortable being around a strange dog but staying on the porch with the Basenji was a lot better than any contact with reptiles.

"Tom, why don't you go ahead," she said. "I'll stay here with Martha and the baby and, er, her." Martha squatted down and rubbed the dog's back, and the dog arched her head up against her hand like a cat.

Dad and Jenny and I walked around the side of the house to the shed, an old single-wide wooden trailer

153

surrounded by peach and orange trees. The hound was chained by the side of the building, his howls trailing off to low groans as we got near. Mr. Yeomans' voice came from inside the shed. He sounded strained and out of breath.

"Sherman, you son of a bitch, cooperate!"

I came through the door first. One look made me glad Mom hadn't come out with us. Mr. Yeomans was bent over a long table and leaning on one elbow, his feet were planted wide for balance, and he appeared to be strangling a very fat, four-foot long brown snake. He had one hand around the snake's neck, his thumb and forefinger on either side of the head. With his other hand he gripped the snake's midsection. The back half of the snake was free and it was wrapped around his wrist and arm, squeezing his flesh up between its coils. Mr. Yeomans gave us a quick smile when he heard us come in, then he turned back to his work.

"Mr. Letour, nice to meet you. I've enjoyed having your son in my class. And young Mr. Letour, if you would, come give me a hand with the nether end of this critter. I'd invite Jenny but she's just not inclined toward snakes."

Jenny made a face and backed away toward the door. Dad moved in a little nearer to look but stayed well out of range. I came over next to the table and listened as Mr. Yeomans talked through the procedure.

"Glad you all came by. Sherman here's almost too big to milk by myself anymore and he's particularly unruly today. Son, you just get a firm grip about halfway between my back hand and the end of his tail. No, use both hands in case you need to shift. I'm going to slide

154

my left hand a little up toward his front and you follow me with yours. We gotta immobilize this guy so he can't coil. Okay, that's better. Now watch; I'm going to squeeze either side of his head to force his mouth open. See how his fangs are out? Hold tight, now. I'm going to force his fangs over the edge of that jar and down through that rubber membrane. This is how we get the venom, and he doesn't like this part at all. There. See that liquid running down the side? He'd sure bite me a good one if he could."

He pushed the snake's jaws down on the lip of the collection jar several times, and each time the snake squirmed and pumped out a little more venom. After a minute Mr. Yeomans pulled the snake's head away from the glass. The snake sheathed his fangs, closed his mouth, and relaxed his body a little beneath my hand.

"That's good. You can let go; I got 'im. You go pick up that long snake hook down at the end of the table. I'm gonna wrestle our friend here into a cage but I want to be ready in case he tries anything funny." He gathered up the snake and together we walked over to a rack of wire-mesh drawers hanging on the wall. He showed me which one to pull out, then dangled the snake over the open drawer and dropped it in tail first. As the snake hit the bottom and started to coil, Mr. Yeomans latched the top down and pushed the drawer back into the case.

The room was quiet and I realized I'd been holding my breath, totally focused on the snake. I looked over at Dad and Jenny. Dad's expression was one of disbelief; Jenny had a half-smile on her face and she gave me a little thumbs-up.

"Pretty good for the first time, son." Mr. Yeomans

wiped his hands on his pants. He turned to Dad. "Mr. Letour," he said as he shook his hand. "Now let's go talk about this dog."

Over iced tea Mr. Yeomans repeated pretty much what he'd said in class. When he was done he asked Dad and Mom if they had any questions.

"I just don't know," Mom said. "The kids want a dog to replace old Chub but it just isn't going to be the same. Chub was big and slow and just so gentle. They used to pull themselves up on his fur; that's how they learned to walk when they were toddlers. He just took it all in stride and it never seemed to bother him. But I'm worried for little Mary. I can't have a dog that might bite, not even by mistake. And we don't have much room in the house..."

By the time Mom had listed all her objections I was pretty sure we'd never get this dog or any other. I looked around the porch at our family. Mom sat stiffly, holding Mary in her lap and looking defensive. Martha sat by the dog, scratching her behind the ears. Dad hadn't said anything since Mom started speaking; he just sat and looked thoughtful. Just when I was pretty sure Mom had killed any chance of a deal, Dad cleared his throat and turned to Mr. Yeomans.

"I was noticing your hound, Old Major is it, out at the shed and I was wondering. Does he always howl this way or is it because this dog's here?"

Mr. Yeomans chuckled. "Sure didn't make this much commotion until she arrived. I suppose 'cause he always had the place to himself, maybe he feels like she's crowding him. He's pretty territorial."

Dad nodded. "And I take it that Old Major is, well, as advertised: pretty old?"

"Oh, I believe he's comin' up on ten, maybe eleven years," said Mr. Yeomans. "We got him from a farmer north of town when he was just a pup so I'm not exactly sure of his age. Why?"

Dad scooted his chair closer to Mom and put his hand on hers.

"Honey, I know you don't have much use for dogs or for animals in general, and to tell the truth, neither do I. I liked Chub but, you know, he could be a real trial. Like coming in from the rain and rolling on the rugs to get dry and smelling up the house and the time he ate a whole pound of butter and how awful he was to clean up after for a couple of days..." He stopped for a minute and patted her hand. "But we survived Chub and I figure this dog can't be any worse. So here are a couple things I'd like us to consider."

I held my breath. Dad's description of life with Chub was pretty accurate and I wished he'd stop talking.

"First thing is, I don't know how long we'll be in Georgia. It may be for only a year, it may be longer, and if I want to stay with the company I won't have a lot of say in the decision. Second thing is, the kids really want a dog. This one here seems to have a lot of things going for her: quiet, clean, gentle around children. Plus we know where she came from." He turned to Mr. Yeomans and continued. "Seems like taking her might be helpful to you since Old Major isn't really happy having her around. Although it also seems like Old Major himself may not be around for much longer." Mr. Yeomans nodded.

"So," said Dad, "here's what I propose. And dear," he turned to Mom again, "this is only if you agree. How about we take her home with us and give her a try. The kids can have a dog, *if* they do a good job of caring for her. If not, she comes right back. Mr. Yeomans, if Old Major dies and you decide you want this one back, or if we get transferred and can't take her with us, she can come back here. How does that sound to you?"

I squeezed Martha's shoulder and we waited in silence. After an eternity Mom looked at Dad and nodded her head. They both looked at Mr. Yeomans. "I can live with that," he said, and smiled. Martha let out a little whoop and I started breathing again.

As soon as we got home Martha started lobbying for the dog to stay in her room, but Mom held firm.

"I said no, so don't ask again. Will, you and Jack can get some scraps from the cabinet shop tomorrow and start on a doghouse. She can stay in the laundry room tonight, but tomorrow first thing, it's outside." Mom started on dinner, Martha changed little Mary and played with her on the living room floor, and while they were busy I poked around in the laundry room, rearranging some of the boxes and shelves. When I was done I had a nice nest over behind the washer, out of Mom's way.

One of the things that used to drive Mom nuts about Chub was his behavior during meals. He was so big he could sit on the floor and rest his chin on the edge of the table and stare at us while we ate. We all used to laugh at this – even Dad – but Mom would glare and whack Chub on the snout and talk about how having a dog at the table was unsanitary. The Basenji, on the other hand, didn't make a sound all through dinner. She sat quietly in the corner with her back straight and her chin and ears up, watching everyone.

"Okay, Anne," said Dad at the end of dinner, "you have to give the animal credit. She didn't beg once and she didn't make a peep. Wouldn't you say she's got class? I think she looks like royalty."

"She looks like a queen," Martha chimed in. "And she's from Egypt, so we should call her Cleopatra!" She bent down and held her hand out. "Here, Cleo!"

The dog looked at the outstretched hand for a moment, then stood up and walked over to Martha and licked her hand once. Then she moved over and rested her head on Mom's knee, her beautiful brown eyes looking straight up into Mom's. After a minute Mom gave in.

"Well," she said, "I think Cleo will do just fine."

## CHAPTER THIRTY-ONE

THE MATTRESS ON THE HIDE-A-BED IN THE TV ROOM WAS old and thin, and the crossbar on the metal frame hit me right in the middle of the back. I scrunched my way toward the foot of the bed, pulled the pillow down with me for some padding, and curled up so my feet wouldn't fall off the end. At least Jack wasn't home yet; when both of us were in the bed it was really hard to get any sleep.

Just as I was drifting off I heard some sounds outside the window. I opened my eyes and listened; sometimes raccoons and possums came through the yard on their way to the swamp. A minute later someone scratched on the screen and hissed, "Psst! Yankee!"

I sat straight up against the back of the couch and waited. Outside the window I could see a silhouette, illuminated from behind by the streetlight. The silhouette moved back out of view, then returned and whispered again, this time a little louder.

"Hey, Yankee, wake up! It's Judge."

I rolled quietly out of bed and went over to the window. Judge was just outside and I could smell alcohol, along with the sharper smell of vomit.

"C'mere, you gotta give me a hand with your brother."

"Just a second." I tiptoed down the hall to make sure Mom and Dad's bedroom was dark, then came back, loosened the screen and crawled up on the window ledge. Judge had disappeared but I could hear the heaving sound of someone being sick. I dropped to the ground and went around the corner of the house. Jack was propped up against the back porch, the front of his shirt and pants covered with vomit. Judge stood over him and prodded him with his shoe to keep him awake.

"Better walk him for a while. He pretty much got rid of the moonshine but you don't want him to pass out on his back. Might choke if he does." Judge poked Jack from the side, keeping well out of range. "Sure don't drink much, does he?" He turned to leave.

"Hey, wait! Aren't you going to help?"

"You take care of him. You're his brother, ain't you?"

Judge disappeared toward the front of the house just as the back door opened and Dad emerged. He stood for a moment, surveying the scene, then he bent down and sniffed. Jack mumbled something about his stomach, turned his head, and threw up half-heartedly a few more times.

"Doesn't smell like beer; more like white lightning," Dad said. "How'd he get out here?"

"Somebody came to the window and told me he

was back here," I said. "Said he was pretty drunk and I better take care of him."

Dad thought about this for a minute. "Go in the house; get the bathtub running," he said. "Then come back out and get him stripped. This should be a good object lesson for you both." His voice was tense and angry.

I wanted to say *What do you mean? I didn't have anything to do with this*, but I figured now wasn't the time to argue.

When I came back outside Dad was sitting on the porch, watching Jack weave around as he tried to take off his pants and shoes. Jack's shirt was already in a soggy pile on the grass. He was cursing under his breath.

"Okay, get him naked, put his clothes in one of those burlap sacks from the laundry room, and leave the bag out here," Dad said. "I don't want any of that crap in the house, and I don't want your Mom having to clean up his clothes. He can take care of it later. Walk him inside and get him into the bathtub. I want you to scrub him until there isn't any smell left, then get him dry and into bed." He looked down at Jack, who had struggled to a sitting position against the house and was breathing heavily, his eyes closed. "On second thought, I don't care if he spends the night on the floor. I just don't want anything else soiled. That mattress is pretty bad but you still have to share it for awhile, so it's your call about where he sleeps. I'll take over in the morning."

He turned and opened the screen door. As he went inside I heard him mutter, "Goddam good thing it's the weekend coming up."

## CHAPTER THIRTY-TWO

I WOKE UP SLOWLY AND DOZED, HAPPY THAT IT WAS SATurday, there was no school, and I didn't have to jump right out of bed. After a minute I uncoiled from my usual position down at the bottom of the mattress and stretched. Something was missing. I opened my eyes and looked around and realized that I wasn't sharing a bed with Jack. Then I remembered last night's events.

The garage door rattled open and I sat up. An engine started and idled for a minute, then I heard our car crunch its way out onto the gravel and stop. Strange, Dad didn't have to work today. What was going on?

"Oh, God."

The voice came from somewhere near the floor. I bent down to look. Neatly placed beside the bed was Jack's new pair of Bass Weejun penny loafers, buffed to a high shine and partially filled with vomit. Next to the shoes was Jack's head. It moved carefully back and forth.

"Oh, God."

He was still covered with the blanket that I had thrown over him after he'd fallen out of bed and I'd decided he was too heavy to wrestle back in. He was also lying in roughly the same position as I had left him, jammed between the dresser and the front of the hide-a-bed. I watched as he pushed himself upright and wiped his eyes. After a minute he closed them again and gave a few half-hearted dry heaves.

Dad appeared at the entrance to the TV room and stood there, looking us over. Jack looked back at him and groaned, and Dad smiled a tight smile. "Up and at 'em, boys, it's a beautiful day! Time for a hearty breakfast and then off to work. There's lots to do."

At the mention of food Jack looked stricken and closed his eyes again. Dad left the room whistling and soon I heard the clink of silverware and smelled the aroma of bacon and eggs and Dad's strong coffee. This kind of breakfast was a rare treat, but the better things smelled the more ashen Jack looked.

"I swear to God if I have to eat anything I'll barf," he whispered. He reached for his throat, touched it gently, and groaned. "I don't think I can swallow."

I left him there and went to get breakfast. Martha stood at the far end of the kitchen with her hands in the sink, cleaning up. She caught my eye, shook her head and silently mouthed, "Ouch."

I was halfway through my eggs when Jack sat down beside me and put his head in his hands. After a few minutes he picked up a glass of orange juice and drained it in one gulp. A look of relief came over his face, followed quickly by discomfort and then panic, and he broke for the bathroom. The next sounds I heard reminded me of the night before and I immediately lost my appetite for eggs. Dad went out the back door carrying a bucket and large sponge. Pretty soon I heard water running from the tap alongside the house and Dad rummaging around in the garage. The sounds from the bathroom gradually tapered off.

"Okay, boys, I've got you all set up." Dad rapped smartly on the bathroom door as he passed on his way to the kitchen, raising another groan from Jack. "Get into your car washing clothes. It's going to be a beautiful day."

"Wait a second," I said, "why me? I didn't have anything to do with last night!"

Dad fixed me with an unsympathetic eye. "Well, this is precisely so you won't ever have a night like last night," he said shortly. "You can think of it as an object lesson—actions and their consequences. Now quit bellyaching and get out there." He went back and banged on the bathroom door again. Jack groaned.

I went out to the driveway and found soap, rags, and sponges sitting beside our car. The sun was up and a warm breeze was blowing from out of the south. At least everything would dry fast, I thought, as Jack appeared and we settled down to work.

An hour later we had finished, and I tidied up while Jack sat out of the sun, his back up against the garage wall and his head in his hands. He moaned softly.

"You okay now? You haven't thrown up for a while."

"Yeah. I mean, no. I think my head's splitting in half. Hand me that hose." He drank deeply and put his head under the stream of water, then leaned back against the garage wall, his eyes closed.

Dad came out the front door and walked around the car, stooping to look behind the fenders and up inside the wheel wells. He peered closely at the windows and mirrors for water spots, then bent down and inspected the whitewalls to see if we'd missed any road tar. Finally he stood back and nodded.

"Good job," he said, "Will, you can go now. As for you..." He pulled a set of car keys out of his pocket and held them out to Jack.

Jack had been pestering Dad ever since we moved to let him take the car out by himself. Now it looked like he'd redeemed himself with a job well done. He stared unbelievingly at the keys and reached up to take them.

"Just move the car back into the garage where it's shady before you wax it," said Dad. "I think two coats should do the trick."

# SPRING

## CHAPTER THIRTY-THREE

Spring. The weather had changed from cold and rainy to warm and rainy with a bit of sun, and near the end of biology class Mr. Yeomans moved us outdoors. His pickup was parked under the trees at the corner of the school yard and we all gathered round, curious to see what was underneath the tarp covering the truck bed. He pulled the tarp back to reveal three large cages, each containing a snake. The entire class took a quick deep breath and backed up a few steps. Mr. Yeomans carefully wrestled the cages to the ground and brought one out into an open area where everyone could get a good look.

By this time all the other classes were over; word had gotten out that something was going on and a crowd began to form. I saw Clayton over on the far side of the group. He glared for a moment and then turned away; he'd kept his distance since the scorpion fight.

"Jeez, I hate it. He does this every year," Jenny grumbled under her breath.

"Does what?" I was confused for a moment, still thinking of Clayton.

"Drags out these damn snakes, is what!" She stood with her arms folded, glaring while Mr. Yeomans picked up his snake stick and slid the cover off the first cage. He fished inside the box for a minute, then he hoisted out a fat, dark brown snake and dropped him on the tarp. The snake bunched himself into a coil and reared up, baring his fangs and hissing, his tail lashing back and forth.

"This guy's a cottonmouth moccasin. He's pretty active today because it's warm, plus he doesn't like being handled very much. See the inside of his mouth— see the white? That's why he's called a cottonmouth. He's one of the snakes you keep an eye out for, try to avoid if you're fishing." The snake lowered his head and tried to slither away. Mr. Yeomans hooked it around its thick midsection with his stick and pulled it back to the center of the tarp, pinning it just behind the head.

"This is where things can go wrong," he said. "'Specially with this guy 'cause he's mostly grown. He's strong..." I could feel Jenny tense beside me. Mr. Yeomans held the hook down with one hand, shifted his weight, reached in to grab the snake just behind the jaws, and got the snake around the middle with the other hand. For a moment there was the sound of a lot of people not breathing, and I heard Jenny say "Dammit!" under her breath. I looked at her; she had her eyes closed. She opened them a moment later, looked at me, and shrugged. "I hate snakes."

Some of the students edged in a little closer. Mr. Yeomans held the snake's head out toward them so they could see the fangs.

"His fangs unhinge just like a rattler's so he can chomp down on his prey. He's not as toxic as the coral snake we're about to see but he pumps out a lot more venom. Maybe he won't kill you, but who wants to take a chance?" The snake coiled and uncoiled, wrapping itself tightly around his arm.

"Now this guy's almost too big for just one person anymore." I could see he was straining to hold the snake steady. He gave everyone a last look before he lowered it, tail first, back down into its cage.

The snake was almost completely inside when it hooked its tail back up over the edge of the glass and gave a sudden thrash, knocking the cage over. Mr. Yeomans steadied himself, kicked the cage upright and wrestled the snake inside. Then he slammed the lid down and stood for a moment, breathing hard. I had been concentrating so totally on the snake that I hadn't realized Jenny's hand was in mine. She squeezed fiercely; I put my other hand on hers and squeezed back. She looked at me and I could see her eyes were wet.

"Goddam it," she whispered, "Why does he have to do this? One of these days it'll be more than a finger..."  I looked at her, questioning, but she just shook her head.

Mr. Yeomans picked up his snake stick, paused, and then laid it down again.

"The critters seem a bit restless here. I think we'll look at just one more of them and call it a day." He carried the cottonmouth's cage off to the side and covered it with the tarp, then brought over two more cages and set them down side by side.

"One of these is a harmless scarlet king, and the other is a coral, the deadliest snake around. Anyone want to guess?" He gave us a minute to compare the two, then pushed aside the lid on one of the cages, reached in with his stick and brought up a beautiful snake, banded in red, yellow, and black. The snake was longer than the cottonmouth but not as thick, and it didn't seem as irritated at being handled.

"Mr. Letour, could you come here, please? I understand you had some experience with a venomous creature a while back and you came out on top." Some of the kids behind me laughed and one of the boys hooted, "Whoooee, Clayton! He done gotcha!" I could feel Clayton's eyes burning into my back as I stepped forward.

"Now I know you've already figured out which kind of snake this is because why would I ask anyone to hold a coral," Mr. Yeomans said. He cradled the big snake gently in his arms. "See here how the colors line up. Just remember that 'red on black is a friend of Jack; red on yellow, kill a fellow.' Mr. Letour helped me milk the venom from a cottonmouth like the one we just saw, so he's earned the right to hold Sadie here. Now, just stand still a minute..."

He draped the long body of the snake across my shoulders and around in front of me. Everyone was silent as Mr. Yeomans showed how to hold the snake, how to support her under the head with one hand and cradle her back end with the other so she'd feel safe. Sadie relaxed immediately. I thought how different she was from the little black garter snakes in the swamp near our house in Shelton. They were slimy and had a bad smell that stayed on my hands when I picked them up. Sadie's skin was cool and slippery, like silk, and she didn't have any smell at all. I could feel the large muscles bunch beneath her scales as she adjusted herself to me. She turned her head to look up into my face and her slow, gentle movements made me smile.

The other students gathered around to admire her. Most of them still kept their distance, but some of the boys came up close and touched her. A few of the bravest ones asked if they could hold her but Mr. Yeomans said not this time; the day was hot and the snakes were too energetic and restless.

When I finally got tired of holding onto Sadie I handed her back to Mr. Yeomans. Soon afterward the crowd of kids broke up and wandered off and I helped Mr. Yeomans hoist the cages up into the pickup. I was starting to walk away when he called me back.

"Mr. Letour, I have a business proposition."

"Sir?"

"You've got a pretty steady hand with the snakes. You want to learn more about them, maybe I could use another person to help, you know, taking venom and such. Any interest in that?"

"Yes, sir!"

"Okay, I'll call your Dad and talk it over with him. If he agrees, maybe you could come out to the farm this weekend and we could give it a try. Then you and I could talk money."

## CHAPTER THIRTY-FOUR

ON SATURDAY DAL AND I RODE OUT TO JENNY'S HOUSE. SHE was sitting out on the porch swing and reading a book when we pulled up. Old Major was sprawled out underneath the swing and she was using him as a footrest. I watched as she pushed herself off his ample body with her bare foot, scratching his side with her toes as she swung back and forth. With each sweep of her toenails he let out a little groan of pleasure and thumped his tail. His mouth was open and he was drooling. I looked at the dog and thought about how I'd react if she did the same to me. Probably just about like Old Major, I decided.

"Snakes, huh," she said, sitting up and closing her book. "Disgusting. Dal, you and I are goin' over to the  mound 'til these idjits're done." She stuck her head into the kitchen and hollered for her Dad. Old Major struggled to his feet and wandered off, looking disappointed.

Mr. Yeomans came out of the kitchen, wiping his

hands with a towel. The smell of bacon and grits hung in the air.

"How about coffee? You take cream and sugar?" I nodded and looked past him into the dining room. The alligator skeleton I had seen on the table earlier was gone, and in its place was a stuffed cobra, fangs bared, twisted around a branch. Mr. Yeomans chuckled as he followed my gaze.

"Trying a little taxidermy on top of everything else," he said. "That's Raj; he died just last month. Had a nasty temper but he made me a lot of money." He handed me a cup of coffee as he contemplated the snake. "Figured it was the least I could do after all the venom he'd produced." He spooned some sugar into his cup and grabbed a ring of keys off a hook by the sink. "Let's go see our little friends."

The trailer had only a simple deadbolt lock set into the door frame. Mr. Yeomans said he wasn't too concerned about theft; he knew all the likely buyers for snakes in the Southeastern states and all of his own snakes were marked, so any thief would have a hard time selling one of them.

"Anybody who's really determined could just bust through this window," He said. "The lock's just so some yahoo lookin' for somethin' to steal doesn't break in and scare himself to death."

He opened the door and flicked on the overhead lights. The place looked like it had when we'd come out to get Cleo, with wire and glass cages stacked high along one wall, but when I took a closer look around I realized that many of the cages were empty. Mr. Yeomans reached under the table and pulled out a glass beaker with a rubber membrane stretched over its mouth, fitted securely in a heavy block of wood. He clamped the block onto the table and turned to look at the wall of cages.

"Okay, let's see now." He slid one of the cages out and set it down on the floor, pulled off the top, and reached in with his snake stick. When he lifted it back out a fat cottonmouth was looped around the hook end, writhing and hissing with its white mouth open and its fangs exposed. The snake twisted itself off the stick, hit the floor, and made for the door and freedom, but Mr. Yeomans pinned its head with the hook end of the stick and grabbed it by the neck.

"Gimme a hand here," he said. "You remember Sherman?" I nodded and took charge of Sherman's middle and tail end, and together we got him up on the table. He seemed even fatter and more muscular than the last time I saw him. I wondered how much longer Mr. Yeomans would be able to control him alone.

"Notice he didn't go for me just then. He just tried to get away," he said. "He's like most snakes—they'll avoid you if they have the chance, but they will turn on you if you corner 'em. Bring him forward with me and we'll get him positioned for milking." We carried the snake over to the collection apparatus and Mr. Yeomans squeezed Sherman's jaw until the big snake's mouth was completely open. Then he placed his index finger on top of Sherman's head, forcing the fully extended fangs down through the rubber membrane on top of the jar. He gave a running description of the process as he went: push the head down, squeeze the jaws, repeat. I could see clear liquid drip from the fangs and down the interior of the jar. He pushed down a few more times until the flow finally stopped, then he lifted the snake's head up to release the fangs and together we walked the snake back to his cage and dropped him in.

"See how that works?" he said. "He's got venom glands by his jaws and you have to put some pressure on to get them completely empty. It'll take a day or so for them to fill up again. So, you all right with that? You feel comfortable handling him?"

"Yes, sir," I said. I wasn't just comfortable; I was excited.

Mr. Yeomans covered the cage and lifted it back in place against the wall. We milked a few more snakes while he explained the business. On the one hand, he said, the market for snake venom was small, but on the other hand there weren't many snake milkers like him, so things evened out with supply and demand. Most of his venom went to the snakebite and antivenin research program at the University of Georgia. He'd worked with them for years and they paid him a premium because they trusted him.

"Problem is, my business has been off lately," he said. He gestured at the empty cages stacked along the wall. "First off, I don't have as many snakes as I used to. The ones I have are getting older and bigger and harder to wrassle, and a couple of them, like Raj, have just up and died. I need to catch more snakes to make this worthwhile financially, but I can't take a lot of time off to do that because I teach and I still need to milk the snakes I've got. Plus it's easier to do the catching with two people. Safer, too. And it's a lot easier to do the milking with two people 'cause, like I said, some of these guys are really strong. It's kind of a circular problem, really."

He tapped the hook end of the stick on the table as he spoke. In her cage across the room Sadie uncoiled in response to the noise and turned her head toward us, flicking her tongue. Mr. Yeomans looked at her and gave a sigh. "You know, I always wanted Jenny to work with me, but she's so scared of snakes she can't stand to get near 'em. She just wants me to get rid of 'em all. I can't, though; there's money in it and there's barely enough of us milkers to supply the labs that make the antivenin as it is. Plus I feel like I'm doing some good in the world, so I'm kinda stuck." He shook his head, then looked over at me and smiled.

"Anyway, that's the situation. So here's my offer. I'll teach you how to milk snakes, then you can help me and I'll pay you part of the profits. We can also go out along the river to hunt for some new ones, and I'll pay you for each one we capture. Whadda you think?"

I didn't have to wait more than a second to reply. "Yessir, I'd like that. I just need to talk with Dad, make sure it's okay with him and Mom. She hates snakes about as much as Jenny, I figure."

Mr. Yeomans held up his hand. "I talked to your father about this before I invited you out here. He said he trusted you to make your own decision and he trusted me to keep you safe. Far as he's concerned, as long as we're working together and you're not out wandering around by yourself in the swamp he's all right with it. You want to think on it for a day or so?"

"No sir, I'm in," I said and we shook hands. "Just

that, um..." I hesitated for a moment. "I did have a question, though. Jenny was pretty upset at school when you were showing the snakes, like she was really afraid for you. And she said something about your finger."

He released his grip and held up his other hand. The first joint of his left index finger was gone. Not a clean cut straight across, either, but on an angle like someone had taken a swing at it with an axe and almost missed. We both looked at it for a moment.

"Let's go in the house," he said. "It's a story with a good moral and I need some more coffee."

We filled our cups again in the kitchen and went back to the den. Mr. Yeomans settled into his old, cracked brown leather chair and I sat on the end of the couch.

"So this was back when Jenny was just a little kid. Her mom had died—cancer; it took a long time—so it was just Jenny and me and she was going through a real bad patch. I was too; money was tight on a teacher's salary and I was having a hard time paying all the medical bills and keeping our colored maid—Diva was her name—to take care of Jenny when I was working. This one morning I was over by the river and I came on a really big coral snake; must have been all of three feet long. I had my stick and padded bag and I felt kind of cocky, finding such a big one early in the day. I'd been catching and milking snakes since I was a teenager and never had an accident. So I picked him up and shoved him in the bag and all of a sudden he gave a hard twist and a lunge and there he was, hanging off this finger by his fangs." He held up his hand and regarded his shortened finger almost with embarrassment.

"I'd studied corals enough to know I was probably

going to be dead soon. The coral venom interferes with the nervous system, and the nearest antivenin, if there was any, was going to be a couple of hours away at U of G. I knew that because I was one of the few milkers in the state that worked with corals, and their lab processed all my venom." He sipped his coffee. I was on the edge of my seat.

"Now there was the possibility that it was a dry bite. Maybe one time out of ten a coral will strike just to get away and it won't waste any venom, especially if whatever's bothering it is too big to eat. But I figured I'd pissed it off sufficiently, 'scuse me, that when it bit me it was the real thing. Anyway, it only took a few seconds for me to digest all this information and make a decision. I grabbed my Bowie knife and, well..."

He stopped and looked over at me. I realized my mouth was hanging open. He chuckled.

"It wasn't a very clean job, but then I was in kind of a hurry. I got back to the house and was fixing to drive myself to the hospital, but Diva had taken Jenny over town in the car to do some errands. By the time they got back I was in pretty bad shape. Luckily the cut isolated the venom in time and after a couple of rough days I pulled through okay. Scared the life out of Jenny, though. She still hasn't forgiven me."

He leaned back in the chair and was silent for a minute. Then a small smile broke out on his face.

"One good thing came out of that, though," he said. "I had the presence of mind to keep the bag closed and old Sherman—he was the first snake I named Sherman, after that Yankee general that burned down Georgia—he didn't get away. I kept him 'til he died five years later, and I milked him hard for the pain he caused me." He contemplated what was left of his finger. "Kind of poetic justice when you think about it.

## CHAPTER THIRTY-FIVE

AFTER A WHILE I GOT PRETTY COMFORTABLE, TO THE POINT of milking a few of the little cottonmouths by myself with Mr. Yeomans just looking on. But when I asked if I could try my hand with one of the smaller coral snakes Mr. Yeomans said no.

"Stick with the cottonmouths. If one of 'em bites you at least it won't be fatal. I sure as hell don't want to have your mama coming after me."

Once the weather warmed up we went out regularly to hunt in the swampy land over near the river, and he'd give a running lecture as we walked.

"We should be seeing a lot of snakes," he said one afternoon. "They come out for the sun and look for places that radiate heat, like the shoulder of the road or large flat rocks. Best time of year for us to pick some up 'cause they're at a double disadvantage; they're still a little sluggish from the cold and at the same time they have to be moving to find food. It's been a long winter for them with nothing to eat." He stopped and motioned with his stick at a mound of brown, sun-dappled leaves beside a rotten log. I looked closely, stooping down to get a different angle, but all I could see were leaves. He stood and waited patiently for a few minutes, then gave the leaves a poke with his stick. A corner of the pile suddenly became a two-foot long cottonmouth that threw itself to one side and slithered away from us.

"Don't worry, nobody sees 'em very well at first," he said. He reached out and hooked the snake under its middle, lifted it up and dropped into his wide-mouthed collecting bag. Inside, the cottonmouth hissed and struck at the cloth bag's rubberized lining. Mr. Yeomans pointed to the rotten log.

"See that hole in the end? Probably his hibernaculum, where he spent the winter. Good to look out for piles of rocks and logs like this. The snakes start coming out in the morning and hang around getting warm before they start hunting. You might see them mating, too. First two things they want after waking up: food and a partner."

We left the ditch and wound our way through the hardwoods by Jenny's Indian mound and over to the Altamaha. For the next hour we picked our way along the river bank, while Mr. Yeomans pointed out a variety of animal signs: deer scat and raccoon tracks and a little pile of bones and feathers that some owl had hacked up after digesting its meal. At one point he stopped and motioned for me to crouch down, then pointed through the canopy of branches out to a sand bar in the middle of the river where a huge alligator lay sunning himself.

"Remember what I said about most animals? How if we run into them, they usually try to just get away? Well, that guy is one exception to the rule. He can run as fast as you can for a short distance, and usually a short distance is all he's gonna need." The alligator swiveled his huge, dinosaur head in our direction, then slid off the side of the bar and into the river. We watched as he swam slowly over to the opposite bank. I was happy to have the width of the river between us.

We hunted for another half hour without any results, then headed back to the house. We were almost to the road when Mr. Yeomans stopped in his tracks and held out his arm. "Look at that," he whispered. He handed me the snake bag and squatted down, pointing with his stick at the base of an old tree that had been uprooted by some past storm. Dirt had been washed out from between the roots and replaced with leaves and other debris and resting on one of the fat roots was a snake, his colors reflecting brightly in the slanting afternoon sun. "Red on yellow," I whispered. Mr. Yeomans nodded. I realized I was seeing a coral snake in the wild for only the second time.

"Your lucky day," he said and moved in. The snake stayed motionless until he felt the stick under his belly, then he twisted away and made a break for it. Mr. Yeomans pinned him behind the head and picked him up for a closer look. The snake was almost as long as the cottonmouth and even more feisty. "He's good sized; just about as big as my favorite coral. Should be a good milker." We watched the snake open and close his jaws, displaying his tiny fangs.

"Corals have a bad reputation 'cause their venom is so potent, but they've only killed one person in the state in the last ten years. Some dumb redneck, as I recall, tried to stomp the thing to death 'cause he hated snakes. Turned out it wasn't as dead as he thought. When he picked it up to fling it, it got him on the hand and that was all she wrote." He regarded the snake with something like affection. "These guys won't come at you. Mostly they just want to be left alone to hunt stuff over by the river, little lizards and other snakes. I've heard say they're cannibals but I've never seen it." He dropped this one into his other bag and tied off the throat of the bag securely. "I think we'll call it a day and go do some milking and we can figure how much I owe you for today's captives."

It was almost dark when we finally got back from the hunt, and it took us over an hour to get the new snakes settled and the old ones milked. When we finished, Mr. Yeomans invited me to stay for dinner; said he'd take me and my bike home in the pickup afterward. Jenny cooked up pork chops, black-eyed peas, and collards, then after dinner she did the dishes and I sat with her dad in the den while he explained his bookkeeping.

"I keep track of each snake and its output. How much they produce helps me know if they're healthy, for one thing. Also I can project out what to expect in revenue." He used his pen as a pointer on the ledger, showing me the entries by name, date, and volume of venom. "I'll keep a running log that shows every time you help me with the milking," he continued, "and I'll pay you each month when I get the itemized check from the university. As for these two new guys…"

He reached in his wallet and counted out money for the snakes we'd caught. For a second I didn't say anything. Mr. Yeomans cleared his throat.

"I know that's not a lot, but…"

"Oh, no, sir, that's not it. I mean, that's really more than I'd expected. Thanks!"

"Well, you did well for the first time, son. I'd like to pay you more. Let's just get this thing up and running and we'll see."

I was shocked at the amount. It was way more than I made each time I mowed the apartment lawns. Most importantly, it didn't feel anything like work. I loved the time spent in the woods and swamps, the excitement of the hunt, the danger each time I cornered a snake and the thrill in my stomach when I made a capture. I could definitely see a job change in my future.

## CHAPTER THIRTY-SIX

WLS WAS PLAYING ON THE KITCHEN TRANSISTOR, COMING
in clear all the way from Chicago. Tonight the station's new DJ, Dick Biondi, was featuring Brother
Dave Gardner and his new hit single, "You're My
Everything."

Jenny's dad was in the den, doing something with
his Confederate currency collection while Jenny and
I sat outside on the porch glider. I had my arm high
along the back, just behind her head, as I kicked the
swing back and forth. My arm had already started to
go to sleep.

The evening breeze off the river blew cool down the
length of the porch. Jenny leaned up against me and
shivered, and I lowered my arm onto her shoulder, trying
to get the blood flowing back into my hand. She didn't
seem to notice as she kept up her observations about
South Georgia in general and Yeomans in particular.

"I can't wait to get out of here. Dad wants me to stay around and do Ag at Tech, but that's too close. I know he hates to think about me leavin', 'cause except for his sister in Waycross, we're it for family here. Wish I knew something about schools up North; I might just apply. Too bad you're no help there, Yankee."

She nudged me in the ribs and laughed and I moved a little closer. She leaned against me and put her hand on my leg. I got goosebumps. Johnny Mathis came on the radio to sing "Chances Are," and I realized that I probably wore the silly grin mentioned in the song every time I thought of her.

"Won't that be lonely? I mean, don't you have anyone you want to be with here?" I tried to be nonchalant but with her this close my throat had tightened up and my voice cracked.

She laughed again. "Why, have you heard something? Like who – Dal? C'mon, Dal's like you, he's just a friend. Besides, I'm way too young to be thinkin', you know, long term."

I didn't say anything. After a moment she turned to look at me; in the light from the kitchen I could see in her eyes that she understood. She pulled back, lifted my arm down off her shoulder and took my hand in both of hers.

"Hey, I didn't mean, you know, 'just' a friend. I didn't mean that in a bad way. I've known Dal as long as forever and he's smart and I like him and that's all. Besides, I thought you liked that Louise Bledsoe."

"Oh geez, no. What makes you think that?"

Jenny shook her head, amused. "Yankee, you can add women to the list of things in the South you just don't get. She's been talkin' it up to her friends how she thinks you're real brave, with the snakes and all, and how you smile at her in band and how you're gonna ask her out. She even wanted me to talk to you, see if you liked her. I told her to do her own homework."

I sat silently and thought about Louise. She was friendly and she was pretty, but she was also the furthest thing from my mind, especially when Jenny was around. Sure, it was good to know that Jenny wasn't choosing Dal over me, but what about "just a friend"? I wanted to be a whole lot more but it seemed like Jenny had just closed the door on that possibility.

Jenny squeezed my hand, breaking into my thoughts.

"Will, you want to kiss me?"

*Will,* I thought, *Will, that's something new,* and then she leaned over and took my face between her hands and put her mouth gently against mine. After a second of shock I put my arms around her, one hand behind her head, moving slowly so I didn't break the mood. We stayed there for a long time, lips together, while I breathed in the smell of her. Then her mouth parted and she kissed me harder; she shifted position and stretched her legs out on the swing, lying across my lap with her arms up around my neck. She pulled my head down and kissed my mouth, my face, breathing harder, squirming. I put my hand on her stomach and pulled her shirt away, then slid my hand up and cupped her breast. Her breath came more quickly and she spoke against my mouth. "Will," she said, "Will, I don't..." A sudden shiver and she pushed at my hand, twisting away. I tried to put my arms around her again but she got both hands around my wrists and pushed herself away from me and sat up. We were both breathing hard and I could hear my pulse thumping in my ears.

"Okay. I wanted to do that and I know you wanted to do that and now it's done," she said, panting a little. "I liked it and I like you but that's all." I started to protest but she held up one hand and touched my face again.

"No, I can't. Yankee, you don't know how long you're gonna be here; might be gone tomorrow if your Daddy's mill says so. The other thing – you don't belong here in the South. Me, I might not belong anywhere else. Plus I'm too young to start any, you know..." She smoothed her shirt and tucked it back in, keeping her distance. For the first time since I'd met her she sounded a little unsure, a little vulnerable. "Let's just be friends, please. Let's leave it there for now."

"Okay," I said. I couldn't think of anything else to say. Johnny Mathis was done and Dick Biondi had switched to a commercial for the new Ford Galaxy Starliner. I could hear her father moving around in the den, shutting drawers and doors.

"Time to get you home," he called out to the porch. I suddenly realized how close we had been to getting caught. Jenny stood up and yelled back to him. Then she pulled me from the glider and gave me a long, full body hug while I tried to hide a substantial erection.

# CHAPTER THIRTY-SEVEN

WHILE I WAS STRUGGLING WITH MY FEELINGS FOR JENNY, I also had Louise Bledsoe to think about. Things had changed with Louise. In history class she had seemed to side with the rest of the kids in her hatred toward Yankees, and I figured those feelings included me. But at the outdoor biology class, when I let Sadie drape herself over me, Louise just couldn't take her eyes off us. She'd stuck around after class and watched, from a safe distance, while I helped get Sadie back in her cage. After all the other kids had wandered away and I was loading snakes into the pickup she hung back, looking at me and smiling when she caught my eye.

I'd been planning to just ignore her. That was easy to do in history and homeroom, since we sat on opposite sides of the class, and school was big enough that I could avoid her the rest of the time. All except for band class, that is, because Louise played flute and I played clarinet and we were right next to each other in the woodwind section.

"I think she likes you," said Dal, sitting beside me in band. He leaned over to turn a page of music and poked me in the ribs with his elbow. I poked him back. Louise giggled and whispered to the girl next to her. Mr. Burroughs smacked his music stand with his baton and rehearsal ground to a halt.

"Miss Bledsoe, Mr. Letour!" He gripped the podium and glared directly at me. "Concentrate, please!" Louise caught my eye and blushed. Dal whispered, "Told you so."

We'd all been rehearsing Mr. Burroughs' original composition for over a month, and we still weren't playing it to his satisfaction. The piece wasn't all that difficult – just six minutes long – and the underlying rhythm and melody were both pretty simple. That was a good thing for me since the woodwinds had to carry most of the tune and I was still struggling with my fingering and embouchure.

But a couple of areas were still giving us problems, starting with volume. Mr. Burroughs wanted to start the piece off softly to depict the water moving along the river, wind in the leaves, and the birds waking up before the sun. His idea was to gradually get louder as we went along, adding one instrument after another as more and more of nature came awake, building up slowly and ending with a huge crescendo just as the sun broke over the horizon. Unfortunately, we couldn't play softly enough at the beginning to be heard, and by the time we were halfway through we were already at full volume with nowhere to go.

The other problem was the percussion section. Most

of these kids ended up in band because they didn't fit into any other sport or extracurricular activity, being too small or too fat or too uncoordinated. But just being in band didn't automatically solve the problem either. They still couldn't successfully finger an instrument or blow into a mouthpiece. They had the same trouble as everyone else – getting too loud too soon – and Mr. Burroughs was constantly signaling them to keep it down. Then they'd get confused and lose their place in the music and we'd have to start over.

Mr. Burroughs whacked his music stand again, but the class was almost over and he'd lost everybody's attention. He gave up and recited his stock lecture: Regionals are right around the corner; success depends on teamwork; everybody has a chance for a seat at Band Camp. By now none of us were listening. We'd had a long and frustrating practice with lots of interruptions, we were tired and irritable, and we'd heard it all before.

The bell rang and the room emptied out. I sat for a moment, pulling the swab through my clarinet to dry it out before I broke it down and put it back in the case. I noticed that my reed was chipped on one edge; that would account for the screech when I tried for the higher notes, I thought. I was loosening the screw that held the reed against the mouthpiece when a hand fell on my shoulder. I jumped.

"Mr. Letour."

Mr. Burroughs had gotten into the habit of touching, sometimes rubbing, my shoulder whenever he talked to me, and sometimes he startled me when I didn't expect him to be there. I noticed he did the same thing to Dal.

He was friendly with other students too, but Dal and I seemed to be his favorites.

"Sir?"

"I need your help. It's about Louise Bledsoe." He pulled one of the folding metal chairs up next to me and sat down. "Well, it's about your friend Dal, too. You're kind of the center of attention here with Louise flirting with you on one side and Dal horsing around on the other." I started to protest but he held up his hand. "Now, you probably don't realize it but I think Louise has a crush on you. You may not be able to do much about that but could you please try to ignore her in class? And tell Dal to hold it down. I know you two are pretty close friends so you should be able to manage him." I nodded.

"Thing is," he continued, "we really don't have a lot of time until Regional and we're nowhere near getting our piece perfect." He paused for a moment and looked around; except for us the auditorium was empty. He pulled the chair closer and put his hand on my leg. "You've shown a lot of potential and progress and I'm seriously considering you for the scholarship, but I need you to help keep order in class. Can you do that for me?" He stared into my eyes and smiled. "I've seen you a couple times riding your bike with Dal and that Yeomans girl out on Airport Road. My houseboat isn't far from the Yeomans' place. Why don't you come out and we can talk about the scholarship?"

I was stunned. I had forgotten that he was going to award the scholarship based on improvement, not just on how well someone played. There was no way Mom and Dad could afford to send me to camp, it was just too much money. Maybe this would be a way to get there.

"Now before I make a decision I've got to do some research; listen to each of the students play individually. Tell you what. Bring your clarinet home this weekend and I'll pick you up at your house after Sunday Mass. We can go out to the houseboat for the tryout. I'll explain it to your parents when I come over."

His hand lingered on my leg, gave it a final squeeze. He stood up.

"Just do me a favor, though. Don't say anything to Dal. I only have two slots and I'm not sure whether he's improved enough to get the other one. Let's just keep this our secret for now."

## CHAPTER THIRTY-EIGHT

Mr. Burroughs picked me up late Sunday afternoon, and on the drive out to the river he filled me in on Miami Band Camp. It was a yearly gathering, he said, of all the most promising band students from junior and senior high schools in Georgia, Alabama, and Florida. The camp was completely paid for – transportation, food, and lodging – by scholarship funds from each state's Department of Education so if I was picked it wouldn't cost my family anything. He said it was a week of intense practice, and it wasn't going to be easy.

"So you can expect long hours and bad food. I figure by the end you'd have a split lip and bloody fingers from so much practice, but my former students all told me it's worth it." He looked over at me and laughed. "You should see the expression on your face; like it'd be a prison sentence. No, I'm just kidding. It's really fun and very relaxed. You'd make some friends

there that you'd probably still have years from now."
He reached over and patted my knee. "I'd be there, too,
so you won't get lonely or homesick."

We turned off the main highway onto Airport Road
and passed Jenny's house on the left. Mr. Burroughs
drove to a small grassy area just off the road to the
right, tucked in among the live oaks and palmettos. He
stopped and parked the car, and we walked a few hundred yards through the woods down to his houseboat.

The houseboat was moored where the Altamaha
made a tight turn, right before it straightened out on its
way east to the Atlantic Ocean. One side of the houseboat was pulled up snug against the bank, and a wide
wooden ramp reached from the bank up to the deck.
On the other side of the houseboat was open water
with enough space to moor a small boat or a canoe. It
looked just like a lot of other houseboats I'd seen: small
and cozy, with unpainted, weathered shingles and a
slanted corrugated metal roof. But when I stepped
inside I found white carpet and plush couches and a
big kitchen running across the back of the boat. A large
picture window looked out from the main room, across
a small estuary and into the woods beyond. Mr. Burroughs told me to relax while he found us a snack. A
minute later he brought out some crackers and cheese
and a bright red drink that he said was lemonade made
with sloe berries.

"It's got a little kick to it, so don't tell your parents."
He laughed. "Now let's get down to business here."

I spent the next half hour running through my part
of the music while he stood over me, his hand on my
shoulder, correcting my phrasing and fingering. When

I still had trouble keeping the volume down to his satisfaction he said he had an idea that might help. He picked up our drinks and refilled them, then brought them out to the deck. I followed along behind.

The deck wrapped around three sides of the boat, with an area in front large enough for a couple of chairs and a thick, waist-high wooden railing at the edge. Mr. Burroughs leaned on the railing and motioned me to join him.

"Best way to explain the sound I want is to show you," he said. "Stand here, up against the railing, and lean out so you can see way down river to the right. See the canopy of trees that goes all the way across, just above that sand bar on this side? You might have to lean out further; that's okay, I'll hold you." He wrapped his arm around my waist and pushed himself up behind me, bending me against the railing and over the water. I had a sudden flash; a memory of Clayton bending me over the table in the cafeteria. I could feel Mr. Burroughs tight up against my backside. Was that a hard-on I felt? Of course not; I had to be wrong. I bent further to look downriver and squirmed to move away from him.

"Okay, clear your mind and think of the sun coming up," he said quietly. "Pretend that it's not over the horizon yet but there's just enough light to change the undersides of those tree branches from grey to pink." He held me around the waist and rubbed my stomach with his free hand. "Think of how slowly that happens, how the pink becomes gold and orange. Just give it time, don't rush, let the change flow over you softly like the river, see? The light gets a little stronger each minute as we stand here. If you give it enough time and don't rush you can see it happen; gradually everything turns from orange to a brilliant shade of red. Slowly, slowly, building up toward a magnificent climax. That's how the music should go. We can't be in a hurry; we have to give it time, we have to savor it."

I twisted to one side to relieve the pressure of his weight; I was uncomfortable being this close to him and something seemed to be affecting my balance. I said I wanted to go inside, and wasn't it about time to be getting back to my parents? After a minute he let go and stepped back.

When we got inside I sat down on the couch, feeling unsteady and a little sick. Mr. Burroughs sat down and slid over next to me.

"I've been watching you and Louise Bledsoe," he said, "how she looks at you. Did you know how much attention she pays to you? I'll bet she'd be a good girlfriend." He put his arm around my shoulder. "Do you have a girlfriend?"

I told him about Jenny and how we thought alike; how much we both loved to read and share things we'd learned with each other. He made a dismissive sound and leaned over to put his other hand on my knee.

"I don't mean a girlfriend like that. You don't need anyone special to talk about school and books. What I mean is someone to be physical with, to make out with. That's even more important at your age. Look at Louise; she's filled out; I can see she's got really nice breasts. Do you ever want to kiss her, rub your hands all over her body...?" He was starting to stroke my knee and moved his hand up higher on my leg. I

hitched myself away from him and pushed at his hand.
I think I may have said, "No, I don't do that," but I
wasn't thinking straight; I felt dizzy and embarrassed
and sick to my stomach.

"C'mon." His smile and his mouth came closer and I
could smell the bitter sweet lemon drink on his breath.
"I bet you could do that with Louise; she must be just
waiting for you to make the first move. You need to
know how to make love to someone like her. I'll bet
she's had a lot of guys touch her, but you could be the
best. Here, it's easy; I'll show you what to do to make
her happy." He slid his hand from my knee up between
my legs, leaned in, opened his mouth, and kissed me.

I threw up.

The bile hit the back of my throat and I couldn't
move fast enough to turn away; I threw up straight
into his face, into his open mouth. He leaped up and
stumbled backward, coughing and spitting, swiping at
his face with both hands. I watched in fascination as
the bright red vomit dripped off his face and shirt and
onto the white carpet. Then I was up on my feet and
moving away from the couch and throwing up again.
Vomit ran down the front of my shirt. I tried to apolo-
gize, but every time I opened my mouth my stomach
heaved some more.

"God damn it! What...? Fuck! Fuck!" He bolted for
the kitchen and came out a moment later with some
wet rags, then dropped to his knees, cursing as he tried
to clean off the carpet. I stood off to one side in a daze,
picking at my clammy wet shirt, trying to keep the red
liquid from dripping onto my pants. Meanwhile Mr.
Burroughs scrubbed the stain down from bright red

to a dull pink, cursing as his efforts spread it over a wider area. After a few minutes he slowed down, then stopped altogether and knelt quietly on the rug. I stood and waited. He got up and slowly walked over to me, smiling, and spoke as if nothing had happened. It was like someone had flicked a switch.

"Well, I think we're done here for the day," he said, his voice matter-of-fact. "Let's get you back home so you're ready for school tomorrow, okay? Here. Wipe yourself off." He handed me a clean rag, went to the bedroom to get a new shirt, then came out and waited while I got the worst of the vomit off my shirt and put my clarinet back in the case.

The sun was setting as we drove back into town. A few blocks from our house he pulled over to the side of the road and shut off the engine. We sat in silence. My wet shirt stuck to me and I was beginning to shiver in the early evening air. I told him I was sorry for throwing up; that I was getting cold and I just wanted to go home. He sat rigidly with both hands on the steering wheel.

"I wonder how I can get that stain out," he said. When I didn't respond he sighed and spoke again, his voice almost a whisper. "I got that carpet just last year in Savannah; a special run to match the furniture. I'm not sure what to do..." I shivered some more.

"Well. We'll have to keep this a secret just between us. I'll tell your parents tonight that you have one of the Band Camp slots and we won't say anything to them about you ruining my carpet, okay? Okay?" I nodded in silence. I was starting to feel sick again.

When we got to the house I begged off dinner and went into the bathroom to wash up. When I was done

I went in to the TV room to lie down. Mr. Burroughs stayed for a while talking with Mom and Dad in the kitchen. I overheard him say he was sorry I was sick – probably just something I ate – but that he was pleased with my overall performance and I had real potential and he was offering me a spot at Band Camp. They were delighted.

Mr. Burroughs came back to see me before he left. He sat for a minute on the edge of my bed, asked how I felt and made some small talk about Band Camp. I kept my face turned toward the wall and didn't say anything, just tried to stay as far away from him as possible. After a while he stopped talking. I waited for him to leave, but he suddenly grabbed my arm and yanked me over on my back, squeezing my face with one hand, forcing me to look at him.

"Listen to me," he hissed. "Don't even think of telling anyone else; not your parents, not Dal, not anyone. You can't prove anything and nobody's going to believe what you say anyhow. Now, either you can make life hard for yourself or you can forget this ever happened. Understand?" He squeezed my face and shook me. "Do you understand?"

I nodded and rolled away. I was tired and angry and I just wanted to be left alone. As he left he called goodbye to Mom and Dad back in the kitchen. I heard them thank him for all he'd done for me and I felt even sicker than before.

# CHAPTER THIRTY-NINE

MONDAY MORNING I FAKED BEING SICK, ALTHOUGH IT DIDN'T take much acting, and I spent the next two days in bed. Mom kept me in the house, figuring that if I wasn't well enough to go to school then I sure wasn't well enough to play outside. Dad was at work, Jack and Martha were at school, Mom was busy with household chores and taking care of Mary, and I was bored. I would have even spent time with Mary just for something to do, but Mom declared her off limits until I felt better, because, as she put it, "We don't know what you've got." I didn't feel like eating, I'd done all my homework and even read ahead, and I'd finished off all my library books. Even Cleo avoided me. The hours crept by, filled with boredom.

Sometimes I'd doze off and dream of Jenny, Louise, and Mr. Burroughs, all tangled up together in ever-shifting scenes. In one dream I was over on the Mound, scratching through the sand and looking for Indian stuff, then the Mound became a sand bar out in the river and Louise was lying naked beside me. She leaned in to kiss me, her hand on my leg, and just then Jenny walked past us and out across the water, looking back with an expression of disgust. I pushed Louise away and tried to stand up, but she grabbed my arm and pulled me down and got on top of me and her face became Mr. Burroughs' face, smiling as he bent over, so close his breath was in my mouth. I'd wake up, twisted in the wet sheets and with a huge erection, ashamed and afraid that someone would see.

As a young Catholic kid I'd always found the whole universe of sexual information off limits. The Church was completely silent about it except to say that sex was bad and if I engaged in any sexual activity – even thought about it – I'd go straight to hell. As a result I was curious and scared at the same time, and I didn't have anyone to talk to. I figured if I brought the subject up with Dad he'd want to know why, and that would lead to questions about what I'd been reading and what I'd been doing with myself.

There was only one time that Dad ever talked about sex with me. It was a Saturday night right after we got to Georgia; Jack was out cruising around with Judge, Martha was reading, and Mom was in the rocking chair, nursing little Mary. I was curled up on the old recliner in the living room, reading, when all of a sudden Dad appeared at the end of the hall and asked me if I wanted to take a ride.

This was unusual. Dad liked peace and quiet after dinner and he almost never left the house in the evening. He also never took any personal alone time with us kids. I couldn't imagine what he had in mind but I wasn't going to pass up a chance to be with him. I grabbed my coat and beat him out to the car.

Dad drove down Macon Street, over past the stockyards at the edge of town, then out into the dark countryside of south Yeomans County. He didn't say a word. After about ten minutes he pulled over at an unmarked crossroads, stopped the car and turned off the radio. In the silence I could hear the high-pitched peeping of tiny frogs in the ditch, the ticking of the engine as it cooled. Way off in the distance an alligator boomed.

By now I was getting a little worried. Why are we out here in pitch darkness, I wondered; what have I done now? Dad rolled down his window, lit a cigarette (which he could never do at home around Mom), leaned back in the seat, took in a deep drag and said, "So, do you ever have wet dreams?"

"Um, well," I said. Dad didn't wait for my answer, which was a good thing since I didn't know exactly how to respond. Now that the question was out there he just barreled ahead.

"Okay, well, don't. And if you wake up while you're having one, just don't touch yourself. If you don't help it along and you don't enjoy it then it's not a sin." This didn't seem to require a response so I nodded and we both sat there in silence, looking straight ahead until he finished his cigarette. He dropped it out the window and then, almost as an afterthought, opened the door and ground the cigarette out with his shoe. "Dangerous out here," he said, as he started up the car. I wasn't sure whether his last remark concerned fire conditions in the woods or Georgia's threat to my immortal soul.

He never said another word to me about the subject.

Others high on my list of people to not discuss sex with were Mom and Jack. Mom, because I was even more embarrassed to bring it up with her than I was with Dad and besides, what would she know about it from a boy's point of view? And Jack, because whenever the subject came up (and that was rarely) he treated it like it was some joke and I was too dumb to get the punch line. I really couldn't see myself sharing my questions with Jenny, for obvious reasons. That left only Dal, but seeing his shyness around girls I figured he was even more clueless than me. And I sure couldn't tell him about what happened on the houseboat.

So I lay in bed and thought about Mr. Burroughs. What had actually happened out at the houseboat? I tried to remember if I had done anything to make him want to touch me but I couldn't think of a thing. After I threw up he'd been really angry, then suddenly calm and cold, acting like nothing had happened. But it must have been something terrible because he said we had to keep it a secret, just between the two of us; I could never tell anyone about what had happened. And if it was all that terrible it must have been a sin.

And if it was a sin, how was I going to deal with it in Confession?

## CHAPTER FORTY

"BLESS ME FATHER, FOR I HAVE SINNED. IT HAS BEEN ONE week since my last confession..."

The air inside the confessional was stale and humid. I had gotten a late start from our house and took the long way to church, hoping that Father Donovan would finish confessions early and close up before I got there. Then when I was halfway to church I got caught in a sudden, heavy rainstorm and had to take shelter underneath some trees in the park. Even with that delay there were still a few parishioners waiting their turn when I arrived, and time seemed to stretch out forever as I stood in line, soaking wet. By the time I got into the booth and Father opened the little window between us I was starting to shiver in my damp clothes, and now, to top it off, there was a lone mosquito buzzing near my ear. I slapped at the insect and tried to collect my thoughts.

"Yes, my son?" Father's voice sounded tired and a little impatient. Here goes, I thought, "Bless me, Father..." I rushed through the warmup of venial sins of anger and disobedience and bad language, and he responded with his usual "Mm, hmm." When I finished off the small stuff I started on my usual list of impure thoughts and deeds, out of habit, then stopped. I realized I hadn't committed any of those typical sins of the flesh during the previous week. Instead I had been too busy playing back the encounter with Mr. Burroughs over and over again in my mind; agonizing over my actions, wondering if I was going to hell.

Father Donovan cleared his throat. "Son, are you finished? We need to move along."

I was filled with sudden anger. I'm not here to confess some awful thing that I did, I thought; I'm here to talk about something that happened *to* me; something that I didn't ask for. And I'm feeling guilty? And he wants me to hurry things up? I gritted my teeth.

"Father, I need your help," I said, and then I told him almost everything. I didn't mention Mr. Burroughs' name or explain why I was at the houseboat in the first place, but I described his attempts to fondle and kiss me and how I threw up on him at the end.

Father Donovan listened quietly right up until I described puking, then he asked me to hold up for just a second. He opened the door to his side of the confessional, looked out into the church, closed the door and told me to continue. When I was finished he blew his nose and sat for a moment in silence.

"There's no one else waiting for confession," he finally said, "so we have some time to talk about this. I need to ask you some questions. You understand, don't you, that anything you tell me is totally confidential, that I can't say anything to anyone outside of the confessional, right?" I said I did.

"Good. You said this person brought you back home after...the incident. What happened then? Did you tell your parents?"

"No, Father. I just said I was sick and went to bed. He stayed for a while and I heard him talking with Mom and Dad in the kitchen, like nothing happened."

"Is this person a member of your family?"

"Oh, God, no! 'Scuse me, I mean, no, Father."

"Son, I know these are hard questions, but I need to understand how you might be connected to this person so I can advise you and absolve you. So, not a family member. Does this person have any authority over you?"

"No, Father, just in class...I mean..."

"It's okay; I'm not going to ask you who exactly this is. I just needed to know how you relate to each other. So, did you initiate any of this activity?"

"No, Father."

"Is there any chance of this happening again; that is, on your own, would you put yourself in another situation like this?"

"No, Father."

"When this occurred, did you enjoy what was happening between you; did you take pleasure in it? Did you encourage it in any way?"

The scene at the houseboat suddenly rushed back and enveloped me. I could feel the dizziness and Mr. Burroughs' hand on my leg; I could smell his breath and taste the bile rising up in my throat.

"Son?"

"No, Father. I was just remembering for a second. No, it was awful; it made me sick."

"You said you couldn't tell your parents when this happened. Can you tell them now, or maybe there's someone else you can talk to?"

I ran through the possibilities in my mind. I thought about the strain between Mom and Dad, the bickering and disagreements that had just recently gotten worse. I thought about how much Mom hated Yeomans. If I told them about this Mom would push even harder for us to leave. That would put Dad in an impossible position because he'd already said there weren't any jobs available other places in the company. To top it off, Mom and Dad were friends with Mr. Burroughs; Dad and he and Father Donovan joked around after church. Would they even believe my story?

Then there was Jack. He and Judge and their friends sometimes made remarks about the non-athletic students, calling them "queers and pussies." The last thing he needed was a brother who fell into that category. And even if he believed me he wouldn't have any idea what to do, either. I'd ruled out Jenny and Dal. What about the police? I tried to picture what that would be like: no one else had been there on the houseboat to see anything, Mr. Burroughs was a teacher, respected in the community, and I was just a kid. It would be my word against his. Besides, he'd threatened to make my life miserable if I spoke up.

Father Donovan cleared his throat and I realized I'd been quiet for a long time. "No, Father, there's no one. You're the only person I've told."

---

There was silence from the other side of the screen. The rain started up again; through the open windows of the church I could hear the splat of raindrops on the palmetto leaves and the hiss of tires on wet pavement. The only other sound was the mosquito, circling somewhere above me. Father Donovan shifted his bulk in the cramped confessional and blew his nose again. I waited.

"Okay, I haven't had a lot of experience with this," he finally said, "but here's what I do know. There are some people who prey on kids, sexually, that is. Do you understand what I mean? Okay, that's what happened to you. Oftentimes it's somebody the kid looks up to; that's why I asked if it was somebody in your family. But it doesn't have to be a family member; might be a scout master or teacher. And sometimes – I know this isn't the case with you – but sometimes the kids come from a broken family or a family without a strong parent figure and they're looking for someone to relate to. You with me so far?" I said I was.

"So, here's where we're at. What he did to you was criminal. Unfortunately, there's no way to prove it." He paused for a moment and let this sink in. "The most important thing to take away from your experience is this: what happened *wasn't* your fault. You didn't do anything wrong; this guy did something *to* you. You didn't commit a sin. There's nothing to confess or to be ashamed of. Do you understand?"

Feelings of relief and anger washed over me and my eyes filled with tears. I suddenly realized my jaw hurt from clenching my teeth. I tried to speak but my breath came out in gulps, caught in my throat. After a minute Father asked, "How are you feeling? Are you all right?"

"No, I'm really mad! I didn't do anything and I don't want any part of this!"

"Good," he said, "you have every right to be angry. This isn't one of those biblical, turn-the-other-cheek things, this is something evil. So, going forward. Can you stay completely away from this person...no, of course, you mentioned he was a teacher. Well, if you don't foresee this coming up again..." He paused. "If you don't feel like you can tell anyone, and if I can't tell anyone because of my vow of silence, then for now we'll just have to keep talking to each other, eh?"

"Yes, Father," I said. I stayed kneeling, waiting for him to assign me my penance and give me absolution.

"I think you've done enough penance on this one to last for a long time," he said. "Ego te absolvo. Go in peace. Keep in touch."

The skies opened up again as I left church, soaking me through, but I hardly felt the rain. I played Father Donovan's words over and over again in my head, and by the time I got home I was shaking with relief and rage. Mom took one look at me and ordered me to bed. A little later she brought me a glass of warm tea, along with the usual lecture about being prepared and carrying an umbrella. She told me that if I wasn't any better by morning I'd have to stay home from church on Sunday and miss the monthly potluck brunch after Mass. Fine with me, I thought. I assumed Burroughs would be there and I couldn't stand seeing him up close.

I couldn't forgive him, and I couldn't forgive Mom and Dad either for not realizing what he'd done to me.

## CHAPTER FORTY-ONE

MOM WAS TRUE TO HER WORD AND LET ME SKIP MASS ON Sunday. I spent the day reading quietly and drinking her honey-and-lemon-laced tea, but by Monday morning both she and I were sick of my lying around the house. I went off to school feeling better than I had in weeks.

In the afternoon Martha and I took our usual route back home through the park. We were almost to the pool when she stopped and reached over to take my hand.

"Will."

"Yeah, I see 'em."

Five of the kids from my homeroom class were fanned out in front of us, blocking the path. Clayton stood in the middle of the group with his hands on his hips, staring at me. Elwood Burris stood next to him.

"Hey, Yankee boy." Clayton's voice was low and flat, almost a whisper. "Nigger lover. Pussy." He put his fists up and took a few steps forward, shuffling his feet on the sandy soil. I put my hands in my pockets to keep them from shaking. My mouth filled with saliva and the taste of bile.

"Clayton, I don't want to fight you." I tried to keep my voice steady so he wouldn't know how scared I was. "What do you want..."

"Nigger lover and a scairdy cat too," he interrupted. "You're gonna wish you'd never come down here." He hawked and spat in the dirt at my feet. Martha grabbed onto my sleeve. I pushed her over to the side of the path away from Clayton. He took a few steps closer to me while the other kids milled around, waiting to see what would happen next.

From behind me I heard the rustle of branches and the crunch of footsteps on the dry grass. I turned to see Jack and Judge standing on the path.

Clayton put his hand up and stepped back, waving Jack away. "This's s'posed to be between me and him! This's nothin' to do with you!"

Jack looked at me and shrugged, Well? I nodded to him. This was my fight; there wasn't any way out of it. When I turned back Elwood had moved over next to Clayton and I could see something in his hand. The next thing I knew Jack had shoved me aside and sprinted past, blocking Clayton off his feet. He continued the charge straight into Elwood, driving his right shoulder up under Elwood's ribs, lifting him and carrying him backwards into the trunk of a huge old oak. I heard the dull *whomp* of a body slamming into wood; the dry snapping sound of a rib giving way.

For a minute there was silence. Clayton sprawled on

his back in the middle of a sharp-spined palmetto and Elwood huddled in a ball, retching, his feet moving weakly in the dirt. The rest of us looked down at the shiny, black-handled switchblade lying on the ground where Elwood and Clayton had stood just moments earlier.

Judge walked past me and picked up the knife. He flicked it open, then closed. "Y'all go on home now," he said as he put the knife in his pocket. "It's over." Clayton rolled off the palmetto and struggled onto his hands and knees. The other kids turned away and started to drift back into the trees when suddenly someone said, "No." It took me a second to realize the voice was mine.

I knew I couldn't just let things go on like this. If I walked away today there would just be another fight tomorrow, and then another. If I didn't finish this nothing would ever change and I'd be looking over my shoulder for as long as we were here. I walked over to where Clayton was kneeling, bleeding from palmetto spear cuts on his arm and face.

"Clayton."

He raised his head. I planted my feet, pulled my arm back and hit him as hard as I could in the nose. He gave a scream and fell on his side with his face in his hands and blood dripping between his fingers. I circled around him, looking to land another sucker-punch, but he struggled to his feet and charged at me, arms flailing. I tried to step aside but I turned my ankle in the sandy soil and he got a grip on the back of my shirt. He pulled me to him, wrapping his arms around me from behind, one around my chest and the other around my neck. I tried to break free but he lifted me off the ground and bent me backwards, choking me. I hammered him in the stomach and ribs with my elbow.

"Fuckin' Yankee bastard!" he grunted.

By now both of us were slippery with sweat and the blood from Clayton's nose, and I was seeing stars from lack of air. I twisted my head over to one side and got my throat in the crook of his elbow, caught a breath, grabbed both his arms and lifted my legs up to my chest. Then I straightened out and drove the side of my shoe down the length of his shin. I could almost feel the skin peel away.

He screamed in pain and loosened his grip. I turned my head back the other way, grabbed his hand, got my teeth around the bone at the base of his thumb, and bit down. He tried to pull his arm free but I ground my teeth into his flesh until I could taste blood. He tried to rip at my face with his free hand. I ducked forward, then drove my head back into his face. There was a soft crunch and a muffled cry and I felt a tooth cut into my skull. He let go and staggered backward, coughing and spitting, blood streaming down his shirt.

For a minute we both stood there, heads down and gasping for breath. Clayton wiped his face with his sleeve and stared at me, his expression a mixture of surprise and pure hatred.

"Y'all had enough, now?" Judge said. "You better..."

He was in mid-sentence when I punched Clayton on his broken nose, then stepped back and kicked him in the balls. He dropped to the ground and curled up on his side. I jumped him and levered him onto his back, straddling his arms with my knees as I hit him in the face. I felt one of my knuckles snap and kept hitting him with my open hand. He looked up at me through his one open eye as he tried to dodge the blows, real fear on his face.

I heard people yell my name but I couldn't stop. This was my chance to pay them all back; Mr. Burroughs, Clayton, the universe. I hit him again. It felt so good. Slap. Don't fuck with me. Slap. Don't fuck with my family. Slap. Clayton was crying, trying to get his arms free to cover his face; trying to roll, to buck me off. Slap. Don't ever...

Then Jack and Judge dragged me to my feet and walked me away from the clearing. We all headed toward home, with Martha hugging me and both of us crying, her arms so tight around me I could hardly breathe.

## CHAPTER FORTY-TWO

MR. YEOMANS TALLIED UP OUR WEEKLY NUMBERS, THEN closed the book on his calculations, picked up his ledger and wrote out a check for my snake activities.

"Thanks, sir." I pocketed the check without looking. There was no reason to; he always paid me more than I expected.

He looked my bandage-wrapped hand and chuckled.

"Heard you had another set-to with that Clayton kid. How's the hand?"

"I broke a knuckle on his teeth but it's pretty well healed by now. I hope that's all over but I don't know; I just don't get it with Clayton. Most of the other kids are pretty friendly, or if they're not friendly at least they stay away; they don't just start fights with me for no reason."

Mr. Yeomans poked at his pipe and relit it, listening.

"But I feel it's not just me, it's the whole family. Well, maybe not Jack; he's on the football team and hangs out with Judge and his friends. But I know Mom doesn't have any women friends like she did back home, and one night I overheard her and Dad talking about the mill; how none of the company wives talk to her and the guys he works with don't invite him out for drinks after work. And even church; I think the only friend she has from there is Dal's mom." I stopped for a minute and took a breath. "I know it hurts her a lot. She really hates being here. I wish I knew..."

"Can't do anything about it," Mr. Yeomans cut in, leaning back in his chair. "Thing is, and this's nothing against you personally, you're a Yankee..." I started to speak but he raised his hand. "No, listen. You're a Yankee. In the eyes of the folks here you'll always be a Yankee. People look at you, they see someone who rode with Sherman across Georgia and humiliated their ancestors; someone who killed their great-great-granddaddy and looted his livestock and burned his farm. And then they hear about the Freedom Riders and they read that the government in Washington is gonna force their kids to go to school with negroes – hasn't happened in Yeomans yet but it's coming – and that just makes things worse. It's no wonder the Klan is getting stronger. You weren't here last Fourth of July but they rode at the head of the parade. Wore their hoods and everybody cheered. Anyway, you've had the misfortune to move here..."

He stopped for a moment and sat, shaking his head. Then he set down his pipe, got up and went over to an old cabinet that sat back in one corner of the den. He dug around inside for a minute, then pulled out a large metal box and carried it back to the table beside his easy chair. He lifted up the top and took out an old brown envelope.

"You gotta understand the war to know why folks around here are resentful, even after a century." He sat down with the folder in his lap. "See, the Confederate Army lost almost every major battle fought on Georgia soil. Sherman came in and pretty much destroyed Atlanta, then he drove his army down across the state to Savannah and on the way his soldiers tore down everything in their path: farms, factories, railroads. You know that long piece of metal wrapped around the big oak in back of the house? Looks like a hunk of railroad track?"

I nodded.

"Well, that's exactly what it is. Yankee soldiers tore up the tracks, built fires to heat them up, and twisted them around trees. Called them Sherman's Neckties. They did it just because they could, sort of a poke in the eye to the people around here. Sherman didn't run up against much resistance toward the end and he burned and destroyed things just to teach the people of Georgia a lesson. He wanted to show them that the Union was in control and the Confederate government couldn't protect them or their families. And he damn sure got his point across. When he got to Savannah the Confederate general that was guarding the city – Hardee, I think it was – took his men and high-tailed it out of there. Mayor opened up the gates and let Sherman in. That was a wise move; he didn't want his city to suffer the same fate as Atlanta. Though nowadays some diehards say that surrender was a cowardly act and he should'a held on to the end."

He sighed, fiddled with his pipe, relit it. "We had some victories over the Yanks early in the war – Brown's Mill, Kennesaw Mountain – but in the end they really didn't matter much. Mostly the war was just a sorry parade of young men, scared and hungry, doing their best to survive one more day and get back home alive. I had a couple ancestors in the conflict. my great-grandfather Jonathon – he was an Army surgeon; some of his instruments are over there on the mantelpiece – him and his brother served together and fought at Doctortown Bridge, a couple miles downriver from here."

He fished around gently in the envelope, then pulled out a single piece of paper inside a cellophane cover and handed it to me. It was a letter, its faded ink and crabbed handwriting barely readable. I held it up to catch the light. "My dearest wife," it began. "The rain has finally stopped and we are on the move once more, not knowing what tomorrow will bring." This was followed by a brief description of living conditions and morale on the day before the fight. It ended with a resolve to "engage the Yanks and prevail, should God give us the means and the opportunity." I handed the letter back to Mr. Yeomans.

"Don't know much about the battle," he said. "Only that Jonathon made it through and his brother didn't. After the war he came back here, took over the family property, raised tobacco and a bunch of kids and practiced medicine. Did pretty well for himself, too; more and more folks moved into the area after the war and they ended up naming a town and then a county after the family." He placed the envelope carefully in the box.

After a minute or so of thoughtful silence he asked,

"You read any Faulkner?" I said I didn't. "He's a local boy; understands the Southern mind pretty well. He says in one of his books that around here, "The past isn't dead, it isn't even past." We're still dealing with folks like my ancestor Jonathon; they're still living out their history a hundred years later and hoping for a different outcome. You understand that, you can keep from being too disappointed in us folks."

## CHAPTER FORTY-THREE

I GRABBED MY LUNCH TRAY, PILED ON AN EXTRA HELPING OF grits, and picked up a glass of iced tea before heading over to sit with Dal and Jenny. As I worked my way through the crowd of students I thought about how much easier things had gotten for me over the past couple weeks. I had already avoided Mr. Burroughs once by not going to church and I knew I could do a convincing sick act at least one more time if I had to. In band class I still had to look at him, but he didn't try to talk to me in a room filled with other kids.

Jenny and Dal had already started on lunch when I got to the table. I put my tray down next to Dal and sat, still thinking. The ordeal with Mr. Burroughs felt like some kind of milestone. I had survived it, and even though I couldn't tell anyone but Father Donovan, at least he was one person who understood and supported me.

The fight with Clayton had been a huge turning

point for me, too. The news about it spread quickly through school and when I came to homeroom the next day there was already a different feeling in the air. Clayton was nowhere around, and when he did show up a couple of days later he had stitches in his lip and two black eyes. There was no more leering, no more "nigger lover" taunts, and his friends, who usually egged him on, were subdued. So subdued, in fact, that Miss MacDonald left the ruler alone.

A few more kids did talk to me, said they had heard about the fight and wondered how I was doing, but no one said much more than that. I figured everyone still saw Clayton as the school's head bully and no one wanted his attention turned on them. Still, I began to relax more around the other kids. Clayton stayed away, Louise smiled and said hi to me between classes, and Jenny and Dal and I joked around more. Maybe I was starting to fit in after all.

Thursday's lunch was the usual fried chicken, grits, collard greens, hush puppies, and red jello. I now knew that kids put pepper sauce on everything but the jello and I thought back to my first lunch in the cafeteria, choking on the sauce and spraying iced tea all over the table as Jenny looked on, laughing.

"Betcha can't do it. Y' still have Yankee taste buds." I looked up. Jenny had a big grin on her face as she held out a slim bottle of Avery Island's Best.

I took the dare, splashed out a large helping all over my plate, and dug in. Dal watched me with something approaching respect.

"Not too bad," he said. "I still say you gotta put it

on the jello, though. Hell, I hear tell Clayton drinks it straight outta the bottle."

"Let him," I said. I slowed down for a moment to catch my breath, then took a huge gulp of sweet tea and swished it around, trying to get the taste of the peppers out of my mouth. It didn't help much. "Jeez," I said, "this stuff is hard on the stomach. I can't believe you have it more than once a year." Jenny grinned wider.

I stuffed down the last of the grits just as the bell rang. Jenny gathered her books and headed out while Dal and I walked across the hall to band. Right next to the auditorium door there was a water fountain, and before we went in I stooped down to get a few mouthfuls. The pepper taste still hung in the back of my throat.

"Wish Burroughs would make up his mind on Band Camp," Dal said as we took our seats. Mr. Burroughs was already whacking on the podium with his baton, trying to get some order and silence.

"Mom's prayin' and keepin' her fingers crossed for a scholarship," Dal continued under his breath, his head down. "Yeah, I'd like to go to Miami. But mostly I want to get this damn thing done and over with."

By 'this damn thing' I knew he meant "Sunrise". At least half of each week's class time was taken up with practicing the piece, over and over and over again, and by now everyone was sick of it. Band morale was low and the music was starting to be a joke outside of class. Just last week one of the girl saxophone players, tired of being yelled at, had just flat quit; stood up and walked out. When Mr. Burroughs met with her parents and tried to smooth things over, as she told the other students later, it didn't help that he told them he yelled at everybody equally. Her parents took the issue to the Principal and demanded she be allowed to drop the class. She got assigned an additional homeroom period.

Mr. Burroughs stood and waited until the room was under control, his face tight. In the silence I could hear my stomach rumbling; I shifted in my seat and tried to find a more comfortable position.

"Okay, people, we've got just three weeks until Regional. Just three more weeks to get this perfect. Today we're going to concentrate on a few of the problem spots and then we'll play the piece all the way through." Dal whispered an obscenity, Louise gave a little sigh of exasperation, and from all over class there were muted groans. Mr. Burroughs glared around the room and waited impatiently for silence. When things quieted down he turned his attention back to his sheet music.

"All right," he said, "go to page four, just before the trumpets come in. Remember how I told you to visualize this; the undersides of the branches are beginning to brighten so we want to bring in a little more volume, but not too much because there's still a long time before sunrise. Okay, ready..."

My stomach clenched as I heard his words, the same words he had used to describe the river scene as he pressed me up against the railing of the houseboat. The memory brought up a little bile in the back of my throat. He rapped the podium and swept his baton downward, and the saxophone section behind us began softly laying the groundwork for the trumpets' entrance a minute later.

Surprisingly, the next half hour of practice was the best we'd ever had. With only ten minutes left in the class we were close to the climax, when, as Mr. Burroughs had explained numerous times, the sun would finally "thrust itself gloriously above the horizon." I began to feel a sense of accomplishment, almost one of pride, creep through the room. We were still a long way from perfect, but for the very first time in extended play everyone was reading the music correctly and hitting almost all the cues. Dal looked over and winked as if to say, "Can you believe we're actually getting this right?"

On the other hand, every moment for me was agony. My stomach was churning and gassy from lunch and there was no way, short of farting, to get any relief. Halfway through rehearsal, when Mr. Burroughs had gone over to the other side of the room to harangue the horns, I had surprised Dal by forcibly switching seats with him so I wouldn't be sitting right next to Louise. By now I had completely stopped playing and was just fingering the notes. I knew that if I tried to blow into the instrument it would certainly result in a disaster at my other end.

I kept my eye on the music, waiting, and when the trumpets came in I rocked to one side, lifting the cheek nearest Dal. The brief blare of the trumpets covered up the sound of my fart but not the smell, and a moment later Dal winced and looked at me accusingly, mouthing the words, "Holy shit!" I gritted my teeth, gave him an apologetic look and shrugged. Louise didn't seem to notice anything and played happily on.

The trumpets had gotten me some temporary relief, but a few minutes later my stomach pains were worse than ever. I let out a couple more tentative blasts. Dal hitched his chair away from me, cursing under his breath, and judging from Louise's pursed lips and wrinkled nose she, too, was beginning to notice that something wasn't right. The music continued to swell and so did I, trying desperately to hold everything in until we could get to the ending.

We had never played the piece through successfully before, but I knew from Mr. Burroughs' description what to expect if we did. At the beginning of the year he had talked about accepting the influence of other composers and finding inspiration in their work. He said that "Sunrise" should bring to mind the volume progression of Ravel's *Bolero* along with the cannons of Tchaikovsky's *1812 Overture*. Since we didn't have access to cannons he had finished off the piece with a sustained kettle drum roll, capped by a furious cymbal clash. It was a simple idea. All it required to be successful was Charlie Echols, who manned the cymbals in the percussion section.

I sat writhing in my seat, saying a silent prayer for Charlie and his music reading skills, and finally the trumpets and trombones rounded the turn, picked up the kettle drums down the stretch and charged for home. They all roared across the finish line together, the sun burst out from behind the trees and leaped into the sky and, in anticipation of Charlie's explosion of cymbals, I finally relaxed.

Charlie missed his cue.

Some of the students said later they hadn't been able to tell when the kettle drums stopped and the fart began. The day was hot and muggy and my cheeks were pressed down onto the sweaty seat of a metal folding chair, so the sound was percussive as well as loud. It completely filled the void left by Charlie's missing cymbals, and it seemed to go on forever. The students sat in silence, clutching their instruments, and Mr. Burroughs stood frozen in place, his baton held high and a look of shocked disbelief on his face. For an instant nobody moved, and then all hell broke loose.

Dal lunged sideways away from me, coughing. He stumbled into Louise, who was struggling up out of her chair, holding her flute with one hand and her nose with the other. The two of them fell over into the music stands. The students nearest to me backed away and fanned the air. There were yells of both disgust and appreciation, depending on the sex of the yeller, and I heard someone chanting, "Yankee did it, Yankee did it!" I got up and just stood there in the middle of all the noise, listening to the applause and boos and Rebel yells, then I headed for the exit. When I reached the hall door I stopped for a moment and looked back. Mr. Burroughs was still standing behind the podium, staring; he hadn't moved and he hadn't said a word. I turned, stepped out into the hall, and closed the door behind me.

After school, and after a lot of teasing and bad jokes from students whose names I didn't even know, I walked home with Dal through the park. He told me how much he admired my performance and how certain he was that Mom and Dad were going to kill me.

"And poor Louise; I think she broke her flute when she fell down, tryin' to get away," he said. "Prob'ly not that keen on you anymore."

"I never thought she was too keen to begin with," I said, turning my thoughts to Jenny and wondering what she was going to say when she heard about it. We weren't going to have any more classes together until

Monday. Maybe I'd ride out to her place on the river over the weekend and talk to her; try to explain. She already didn't have any interest in me as a boyfriend and I was sure this latest incident wasn't going to help my cause any.

Dal's voice interrupted my thoughts. "There's Judge. Wonder what he's up to."

I looked up and saw the Grey Ghost sitting near the edge of the park. As we got closer to the car Judge's hand came out of the front window and flicked a cigarette into the ditch. He waved us over.

"Hey, Yankee," he said, "heard you blew up old Burroughs' class." I heard some muffled snorts; inside the car a couple of Judge's older friends were bent over, punching each other and laughing. He told them to shut up. "That's almost enough to make you an honorary Reb," he continued. "Couple of us are gonna climb the water tower Saturday morning. Wanna give it a try, show us if you're good enough?"

I took a second to consider how things had been going lately.

"What the hell," I said. "Why not?"

## CHAPTER FORTY-FOUR

TEN O'CLOCK SATURDAY MORNING AND THE DAY WAS already blazing hot. Dal and I sat on the edge of his porch and looked at the old water tower across the street. Boy appeared out of the bushes at the base of the tower, wandered over and peed on a corner post of the porch, and crawled underneath to get out of the sun. I leaned down and watched him stretch once, then roll onto his side and lie motionless in the sand. Why was it, I wondered, humans made such a big deal about everything? We should all be more like Boy; just find a cool place, flop down, and call it good.

After a few minutes of quiet Dal said "Dammit!" under his breath and slapped a mosquito. He picked the bloody remains off his leg and wiped them on the porch, then scratched the side of his leg vigorously. We returned to looking at the tower.

"You ever do this?" I asked.

"Naw. Well, I tried last year but I chickened out when I got to the bottom of the tank part. Mom damn near killed me when she found out." He shivered a little and shook his head. "I hate bein' up that high. You?"

I thought back on my history with trees and heights, and I realized being way up in the air didn't bother me at all. Jack and I used to shinny up the young swamp elms across the street from our house back in Shelton, and when we got to the top we'd sway back and forth until the trees bent almost to the ground. The neighbor lady used to call Mom and say, "The monkeys are up in the trees again." And one time Dad brought an old rope ladder home from the mill and helped us hang it in the red oak by the creek. Everything was fine until Mom caught us jumping into the creek from a branch about ten feet up.

"Sometimes I don't know where you two store your brains," she had said. "Your father, too." She kept an eye on us through the kitchen window as we reluctantly took the ladder down.

I looked up at the water tower again. Basically, it was a tank about thirty feet tall, balanced on top of four legs that were also about thirty feet tall. At the top of the tank, a small ragged white flag moved in the early morning breeze.

"Never tried anything this high but it doesn't look too bad. Just gotta make sure Jack doesn't say anything to Mom or she'll have a cow. It's gonna be bad enough when she and Dad hear about band."

I had expected some sort of reaction from Mom and Dad once Mr. Burroughs gave them a call. Neither of them had said anything on Thursday after school. Nothing when Dad got home late Friday night, either, and I was tired of waiting for the hammer to fall. I didn't plan to bring the matter up myself, but I wanted to get the ordeal over with. I figured I had a good enough excuse for the disruption because of my stomach, but I wasn't sure I could explain ignoring Mr. Burroughs and walking out of class.

I thought again about the fact that Mom and Dad hadn't said anything, and suddenly it hit me. Mr. Burroughs hadn't told them. He was afraid to tell them. I remembered how he'd looked at me when I just got up and left class. There was more than rage on his face; there was also a look of uncertainty and now I knew why it was there. He was actually afraid of me. He knew he'd have to be careful about any punishment because he wasn't sure what I would do or who I would tell about the time on the houseboat. I was digesting this piece of information when Judge drove up.

"Well, you sure stunk up old Burroughs' class," he said again, lighting a cigarette as he climbed out of the car. "Never would've expected it from a proper Yankee." He leaned against the front fender. Two other kids got out and draped themselves on various parts of the car, following his lead. "Heard you walked out of his class, too. That took some balls. Wonder why he didn't do anything." He looked at me and raised an eyebrow. I didn't know what to say so I didn't say anything. That was the problem with having a secret, I thought; it could turn even the simplest question into a trap. He finally looked away and motioned at the water tower.

"This one takes balls, too, y'know," he said. "Sure y'wanna try?"

I nodded. I had heard kids talk about the water tower ever since we got to Yeomans. It had been part of the Confederate supply lines during the Civil War, when cattle were shipped north from Florida to feed the soldiers. At some point it provided water for the local stock yard. Now it hadn't been used for years and it was rotten, covered with kudzu, and completely unsafe. The city had put up a high chain link fence around the bottom and posted warnings to keep kids away, and the kids responded by figuring out ways to get through the fence. "Climbing the tower" had become a rite of passage, reserved mostly for the senior class. The ultimate prize was the white flag at the top, but Dal said no one had gotten near it for years.

Judge finished his cigarette and threw it down on the dirt. We all followed him across the road and pushed our way through the undergrowth. About ten feet in we came to a spot where someone had pulled the chain link fence away from its post. We slipped through the opening and stepped over a low concrete wall that circled the base of the tower, about three feet out from the legs.

The whole area underneath the tower was thick with clematis, honeysuckle, and wild rose. Kudzu vines had gotten a firm grip on the legs and from there had crawled all the way up to the tank. Thick horizontal wooden beams linked the legs securely to each other about halfway up their height. I looked for a ladder but there wasn't one, just a series of short boards nailed into one of the legs and going up as far as the beam. Up higher, where the legs supported the tank itself, I could see the underside of a walkway that circled the bottom of the tank. The walkway had a hole in it near the top of one of the legs. Hanging from the hole and tangled in the kudzu was a long, knotted rope that reached all the way down to one of the crossbeams. The whole structure was unpainted and looked ready to collapse.

Judge pointed up. "The rungs on this leg'll get you up as far as the beam. You just need to get across it to the next leg and then it's a short shinny up that rope. You make it up through the hole to the walkway and you can get to the top." This all sounded way too easy. I must have looked at him strange because he added, "You'll see how when you get there."

"You ever do this?"

"Only once to the top; it was awhile back." For the first time I saw a smile on his face. He punched me on the shoulder. "Hell, Yankee, most kids don't even get halfway up and you'll probably fall off anyhow. Wanna quit now?"

I waved him off, walked over to the leg, and jumped up to grab onto the lowest board. The wood was dry and the short board rotated around its nail. I grabbed it with both hands to keep it from twisting, then pulled myself straight up and clamped my knees onto the leg. A couple more pulls and I was able get a foot up onto the board. The rest of the way up the leg was easy, as long as I kept my hands and feet close to the nails. When I reached the beam I stood for a minute to catch my breath and I heard Dal call out, "All *right!*"

I looked across the beam to the next supporting leg, about thirty feet away. There was a brace that angled down from each leg, attached to the beam about six feet out from either end, but beyond that there was nothing to hold onto. I eased myself away from the leg and shuffled toward the far end, arms outstretched, trying not to look down. The beam was dry and cracked and it swayed from side to side as I inched my way along. I was almost to the brace at the other end when a long splinter caught my tennis shoe and pulled me off balance. I pitched forward, hit the beam hard and rolled over the side. There was a searing pain in my left palm, but I hooked one leg over the beam and hung there like a sloth. From down below I heard an intake of breath and someone said, "Oh, shit!"

I closed my eyes and rested for a minute, taking stock. When I opened them I saw a thin line of blood trailing down my arm and dripping off my elbow. Must have caught a nail, I thought. I could sure use that as an excuse to quit. It'd be easy; I was only about fifteen feet up and if I just let go the bushes would break my fall. Besides, Judge said no one had made it up the tower in years.

On the other hand, I only had a few more yards to go and I could grab hold of the next leg.

"How're y'doin', Yank? Y'wanna give up?"

Fuck it, I thought. I hung upside down and hitched myself over to the next leg, where I could grab the rope and pull myself up. A few minutes later I was standing on the beam again, leaning against the tower leg, wheezing and shaking. My hand hurt, all my muscles ached and I was having trouble catching my breath. This was a lot harder than I had expected.

"Y'okay up there, Yank?"

"Just takin' a short break," I panted, "don't rush me, okay?" I looked at the rope that dropped down from

the walkway and tangled in the kudzu vines below. It
looked worn and frayed but there were big knots every
so often, good for footholds.

"So how old is this?"

Judge's voice came back. "Just put it up just last
year; hung it myself."

I grabbed the rope, put both feet on one of the
knots and bounced up and down. There was a little
give but it felt secure. I started the climb.

Winter had killed the kudzu leaves, leaving the
vines bare except for some green spring buds. Both the
vines and the rough rope dug into the cut on my hand
and I had to stop every so often to wipe the blood onto
my pants. It took me almost ten minutes to climb up to
the hole in the walkway. When I finally got there the
opening was almost completely choked with kudzu.
I jammed my arms and legs into the tangle of vines
and hung for a minute, resting. Then I forced my head
between the vines, inching my way up through the
opening, my feet straining against the knots. I pushed
one arm through, then the other, then my shoulders,
and finally I wrestled my body up clear of the hole and
collapsed onto on the narrow wooden boards. From
down below there were shouts of "All right!" and "Go,
Yankee!" I curled up in a ball, too tired to call back,
trying not to puke.

After a few minutes I opened my eyes and struggled to a sitting position. I shifted my weight on the
creaking boards, leaned back against the tank and
let the hot sun dry the sweat on my face. From off in
the distance I could hear a few faint sounds: the noon
whistle out at the mill, the 'scree' of a circling hawk.

Otherwise the silence was so complete it left a ringing in my ears. I closed my eyes again.

"Gettin' tired of waitin' here, Yankee. Whaddaya gonna do?"

I got to my feet, yelled down an obscenity, and turned around to study the water tank. Up close I could see it was made of long wooden staves running from bottom to top, like a huge, black whiskey barrel. The staves were held in place by heavy iron bands that circled the tank about every two feet, connected end to end by huge turnbuckles. The bands themselves were snugged up tight against the tank, but behind each turnbuckle was about an inch of empty space.

I smiled; Judge had said I'd know the way to the top when I saw it. I put one foot on a turnbuckle, reached up to grab another. My fingers fit perfectly in behind the metal. I leaned out and craned my neck; high above me I could see the tattered white flag flapping at the tank's edge. Another foot up, another hand...

"Yankee! Yankee, y'gotta c'mon down!"

"Just a sec." What the hell did he mean, come down?

"Will!"

Oh, shit. Jack. I hadn't told him I was going to be here and the last thing I needed was for him to tell Mom and Dad.

"Will! The fuck you doing?" His voice sounded frantic.

I jammed my fingers back behind the metal, got a good grip, and looked down over the walkway to the undergrowth below the tank. By now there were seven or eight kids milling around. Jack stood on the edge of the group, waving his arms and yelling. I leaned out to wave back and caught a glimpse of red down by my foot. Must still be bleeding a little, I thought. I shifted my balance and felt my foot slip sideways off the metal.

There was a tearing pain in my fingers. The sky and the clouds swung above me, and a second later I landed flat on my back on the walkway, a foot from the hole and a foot from the edge. I am the luckiest guy in the world, I thought as I lay there, trying to catch my breath and also trying to not throw up.

And then the walkway collapsed.

## CHAPTER FORTY-FIVE

I WOKE WITH A START, STIFLING A SCREAM AND CLUTCHING my armrest as the plane banked sharply. My seatmate put his hand on my arm.

"You okay? You want the stewardess or something?"

I shook my head. He shrugged and turned away and I sat back in my seat, fighting feelings of panic and nausea as I remembered cartwheeling through the air, tearing through the kudzu vines on my way from the walkway to the ground. By the time I got my breathing under control the plane had straightened out on final approach into Yeomans Airport.

Where fields of corn and tobacco had covered the landscape fifty years earlier, there was now a sprawl of parking lots and concrete buildings, their roofs painted over with Walmart and Costco logos. I tried to find the long curve and blue-green sparkle of the Altamaha, but thick stands of pine trees covered the landscape like a blanket, blocking the river from view.

The plane touched down and bumped to a stop on the runway, and I stepped out into the warm, humid air of a Georgia afternoon. The old double-wide trailer still served as a tower, but another trailer module had been tacked on one end to protect passengers from the elements, and the resulting "L" shape had been painted a brilliant yellow to cover up the original army surplus khaki. Close by the building sat a canvas pavilion sheltering three weather-beaten Chevys. A faded sandwich sign advertised "Rent-4-Less" and a painted arrow pointed toward the tower building. I picked up my overnight case and went inside.

Five minutes later I drove past the old Yeomans place, and ten minutes later I pulled up in front of The Blue Lake Motel. The pastel cottages were now chalk white, and a faded sign between the office and the highway advertised "Free Cable TV" and "Businessman's Accommodations." I walked across the gravel parking lot to The Pig next door. The restaurant's roof was still covered with multi-colored three-tab shingles, still firmly in the grip of kudzu vines, and fifty more years of foot traffic had worn the groove almost halfway through the heavy lumber of the porch steps. A blaze of neon signs framed the door, announcing the Georgia Lottery, ATM, and Cold Beer.

The gift shop still took up the far back corner, with signs and swords and ancient rifles still hanging on the knotty pine walls. The booths were still covered with naugahyde—the faded pink replaced by faded turquoise—and the dinner special was still chicken fried steak, grits, and green beans with homemade blueberry pie and coffee for dessert. I ordered the special. The coffee came with plastic containers of fake cream and artificial sweetener, the only bow to progress in half a century.

When I was finished I asked the waitress if she remembered Dal's mom. She thought for a minute and then said no, but the manager might. I lingered over my coffee until the manager arrived, a tiny white-haired woman. I identified myself as a boyhood friend of Dal's, just traveling through. She looked me over hard, no doubt mentally refighting the War Between the States, and finally concluded that I meant no harm even though I was obviously a Yankee.

"I do remember Miz Lorraine; used to finish out her shifts for her toward the end, when her arthritis got actin' up too bad. She quit workin' maybe twenty or so years back, passed prob'ly ten years ago. I'm for certain she never got over her son goin' the way he did. Such a terrible loss, I just don't know..."

After a little more local history and reminiscing she gave me detailed directions to Pinehurst. I thanked her and just before I left I asked about the alligators out back. She shook her head sadly.

"Nope. All gone years ago, thanks to them tree huggers an' that dang SPCA."

I headed west with the sun low in the sky and shadows lengthening out beside me. I remembered Father Donovan's complaints about his mobile ministry and expected the trip would be a long one, but the highway was in good condition and I reached Pinehurst in less than an hour. The nursing home was just at the city limits—a three-story antebellum structure standing on a low hill a few hundred feet off the road. It was surrounded by a grove of huge oak trees and attached to each side of the building were low, modern one-story additions. I walked up onto the wide front porch. A sign beside the main entrance announced the visiting hours and I saw I wasn't going to have much time.

Inside the overhead lighting was dim. Aides quietly pushed food carts down the hall, cleaning up after supper, busy with the evening rounds. Just inside the front door to the left was a gathering of coffee tables and reclining chairs, illuminated by some floor lamps, and to the right was a nursing station with a raised counter. The nurse on duty finished her phone call and looked up, a wary smile on her face. "Kin I help you?"

I introduced myself, said that I had been told to contact Mrs. Jessup, and started to explain my situation. When she heard the supervisor's name the nurse relaxed a little. She reached across her desk to a bulky chart and checked some notes just inside the front cover.

"Miz Jessup's got evenings off, but she did leave instructions in case you showed up while she was gone. Please come this way."

Room 114 was at the far end of one long corridor. The nurse motioned for me to wait while she checked inside. She came back out almost immediately.

"I've been told this visit's important, but it's gonna be tiring," she said. "Just try to be quick, okay?"

I slipped inside and pulled the door shut behind me. The room was dark, the only light coming from a small bedside lamp and a muted television screen that flickered in the corner. There was the sour smell of illness and decay hanging in the air. I crossed the room and looked down on the shrunken figure lying in the bed.

"Hey, Yankee."

"Judge!" I stepped back, my mouth hanging open. "Jesus Christ, I didn't..."

Judge laughed weakly, choked, and lapsed into a coughing spasm, his chest heaving under the thin sheet. When he finished he pointed to a glass of water. I handed it to him and he drank slowly, holding the glass to his chest between swallows. Then he motioned me toward an old leather Barcalounger next to the bed. I sat and waited, and when he spoke again his voice was shallow and tortured.

"Expecting Jenny, huh?" he rasped. I nodded. "Yeah, sorry about that. I figured you might not come if you knew it was me. I got a bunch of things you need to know."

"So, Jenny, is she, I mean..." I knew the answer before he spoke and my heart sank.

"Yeah, gone last year, breast cancer. The two of us were just unlucky that way. Blame the smokes for mine." He gave a small chuckle and caught himself before another coughing fit took over. "But before she went she made me promise to tell you everything. Just a sec."

He rang the bedside buzzer and waited impatiently until a nurse came through the door. "Darlin', I believe I'll have another now." The nurse nodded and returned a moment later with a syringe. "Gotta keep ahead of the pain," he said. "Not like I've gotta worry about getting addicted. Gimme half an hour or so and I'll be ready. There's a lot to talk about." He stopped the nurse as she finished the injection and was turning to leave. "Honey, this guy can stay as long as I need him to, okay?" She nodded and slipped out the door. Judge shifted his weight and grimaced. "Fuckin' cancer. Help me with these pillows, then you go get a cigarette or whatever. I gotta rest first."

The cafeteria was closed, but the night shift supervisor poured me some coffee from the pot at the nurse's station, gave me a blanket, and showed me to a lounge chair out on the covered veranda. After a few exploratory sips I put the coffee aside, pulled the blanket over me and closed my eyes. Off in the distance I could hear "Uh hoo, hoo, hoo," a warning to all that a great horned owl waited somewhere in the dark, invisible and hungry. A soft breeze blew through the screen, clearing away the smells of antiseptic and infection. I closed my eyes; my thoughts returned to the water tower and how very close I'd come to death.

In my dream we were back on Jenny's porch and the glider had come to a stop. I felt around with my foot for Old Major so I could push off of him and get the swing going again, but he was gone. In the darkness Jenny's lips were on my cheek, her hair against my face. I tried to lift my arm, to put it around her and pull her to me, but it was numb and too heavy to move. I tried again but the numbness had turned to pain and now someone was sitting on my arm. I closed my eyes and tried to will the hurt away...

I drifted in and out of sleep and woke to a light breeze and the sounds of traffic in the distance. I took a deep breath and forced my eyes open. My left eye felt sticky; when I reached up to wipe it clear I found my head was wrapped in gauze. I turned my neck carefully and felt around. Someone was still sitting on my left arm. I reached over with my right hand to find my left hand wrapped in a bandage and my left arm in a cast. I lifted it up to get a better look and my arm exploded in pain and now I couldn't see for the tears. Jesus Christ...

"Dad, he's up!" Jack's voice.

No, he's not, I thought. I went away again...

The next time I came to someone had cranked up the head of the bed and I could see around the room. Outside the window everything was dark; inside the only light came from a bedside lamp, turned down low. There were faint bells and some muffled voices, the squeak of a cart as it wheeled past the door.

I looked around. Jack was gone, but at the other end of the room Dad lay back in an armchair, his eyes closed and his feet propped up on an end table. The door to the hall opened and Jenny poked her head in, hanging back until I gave her a wave. She tiptoed over and looked down at me in silence. I waited to hear how worried she had been and how much she cared for me, and after a moment she leaned down and put her lips against my ear.

"Yankee," she said, "that was just bone stupid." She stepped back and smiled. "Still and all, I'm glad you aren't dead. I'd miss bein' able to win every argument." She gave me a kiss on the forehead and patted my hand.

Dad's chair scraped as he got up. Jenny gave my hand a good-bye squeeze and slipped out, waving to Dad as she went by. He waved back, then came over and stood by my bed. He put his hand on my shoulder and smiled tightly, then he cleared his throat a couple of times and said how disappointed he was in my judgment and asked who put me up to it in the first place.

"Dad, can we talk tomorrow?" I was too tired to explain. "Right now I just want to know what's broken, okay?"

Dad nodded. He left the room and came back a few minutes later with a night shift doctor who checked out my pupils and reflexes and asked me a couple of questions. He told me I'd been unconscious for about a day and a half, mostly because of the drugs they'd used to knock me out so they could set my broken arm, sew up my scalp and work on my hand. Two of my fingers had been caught behind the turnbuckle when I fell. Both of them were broken and my little finger had been torn almost completely off at the second joint. He doubted that I'd ever have full use of it again. Other than that, he said, I was in great shape and damn lucky.

Well, I thought, if the fart hasn't ruined my chances for Band Camp, this sure as hell will.

I slept for twelve hours straight after Dad left. The doctor had said there might be some discomfort as the drugs wore off; I woke up in the late morning feeling like someone had used me for a punching bag. The hospital wanted to keep me another day for observation so I spent my time alternately pacing the room and lying around in bed. Mom came for a short visit around noon and brought baby Mary, who took one look at me and started howling. I already felt terrible about worrying Mom and she didn't make things easy; every time I tried to explain she just looked at me, sighed, and said, "Oh, William...," and then I felt even worse. She and Mary finally left and I spent the rest of the day alone.

In the early evening a young doctor came by to check me over. He said the stitches in my scalp and cuts across my face would take a while to heal, but the big bandage on my head could come off before I left the hospital the next day. The dressings on my hand would have to be changed every couple of days until my fingers healed and that would probably take two or three weeks. The worst injury was to my arm but even that was pretty straightforward; I had a clean break right above the wrist and with luck I could have the cast off in a little over a month. When he was done he looked at me for a moment and shook his head. I braced myself for another observation about stupid decisions and sheer dumb luck.

"Only got halfway up the rope myself, back in high school," he said. "Couldn't handle all the damn kudzu." He shook his head admiringly, smiled and left the room.

Dad came by to see me on his way home from work. I just nodded when he said I'd been foolish and reckless but when he tried to put the blame on Jack I stopped him.

"Dad, the whole thing was my idea. I didn't tell Jack about it. I still don't know how he found out, but when he got there he tried to make me come down. And Judge was just there to watch over me, like Dal. Nobody pushed me into this."

It was all mostly the truth. I wasn't about to go into how I came to climb the tower in the first place; apparently he and Mom still hadn't heard about band class.

After getting out of the hospital and spending a couple

days at home I returned to school to find that I was suddenly very popular. Almost killing myself had totally overshadowed the band incident. While a lot of the guys really appreciated the famous fart, and told me so, I'd made a lot more points by falling off the water tower.

"Hey, Yankee, how far up didja git?"

"Geez, that's one ugly lookin' face, huh?"

"Can I sign your cast?" That last was from Louise Bledsoe. I told her it was okay and she went at it with colored pencils in shades of pink, even hiding a small, smiling heart on the backside of the elbow.

Jenny was unimpressed by all the attention and told me so at lunch.

"Stupidest damn thing I've ever seen, and I've seen a lot." She rolled her eyes as she dumped pepper sauce all over her collards. "If they gave out medals for dumb..." I was finally getting to where I no longer took her seriously. Still, she was more than a little irritated at me for letting Louise "scribble all over your cast," as she put it.

"You let her do that, then it's...That's like a dog pissin' on its territory, Yankee." She poked at the pink heart. "Where's your respect?"

I sprinkled some of the fiery sauce on my grits. Not too much, this time. "Jenny, I do believe you're jealous."

"Hummph!"

I was almost grateful for the damage to my fingers; it meant I couldn't play the clarinet and that was a perfect excuse to skip band and stay away from Mr. Burroughs. The last week of school I stayed late each day and helped Mr. Yeomans get the biology trailer ready to close up for the summer.

"How's that arm? Cast should come off soon, eh?"

I stopped cleaning out an empty cage near the bottom of the trailer wall and stood up, flexing my arm inside the cast. It was coming along so well that it hardly even hurt any more.

"Itches like crazy but Doc's going to cut it off in a couple weeks. I should be ready for snake catching any time."

The week before, one of the hospital nurses had put me through a series of hand exercises, wiggling and clenching and stretching. I was starting to get some feeling back in my ring finger; I could close it almost completely, but the little finger was still floppy and numb.

"Were you plannin' a career in the orchestra, son?"

"Um…no, ma'am."

"Good."

With only one arm and hand I was pretty slow, but I could still help clean up the living wall and the cages. Mr. Yeomans didn't seem to be in any hurry and I enjoyed the work. Sometimes he brought Sadie in from the trailer and I carried her on my shoulders while I went around watering the plants. While we worked Mr. Yeomans shared a constant stream of stories about the South and the Civil War, from tales about gold looted from the Union paymaster wagons by the rebels to how the Yankees captured Confederate President Jeff Davis over near Irwinsville, when he tried to escape wearing his wife's nightgown as a disguise. Sometimes he'd recite part of a poem and challenge me to complete it, and sometimes, thanks to Mom, I could.

As school drew to a close I spent less and less time with Dal. He'd gotten one of the scholarships to Band Camp and said he was practicing a couple of hours a day to get prepared. He told me that he'd also gotten more involved with the scout troop, and he was helping Mr. Burroughs with the younger scouts when they went on summer camping trips and overnights.

My relationship with Jenny had changed, too. Now that the whole kissing/boyfriend issue had been settled (at least to her satisfaction), she was less prickly and a lot easier to be with. She still teased me about how Louise Bledsoe had a crush on me. I had to admit she was right but I just couldn't get excited about Louise one way or the other. I'd taken her to the movies a couple of times and we'd made out in the back row of the balcony, but when I tried to get to second base she squirmed away and wouldn't let me touch her. When we weren't making out I couldn't think of anything to say, and I'd gotten tired of listening to her talk about which of her girlfriends was having what trouble with which boyfriend.

But the worst part was that whenever I closed my eyes to kiss Louise, all I could see was Jenny's face.

# SUMMER

## CHAPTER FORTY-SIX

SUMMER ARRIVED. WITH DAL GONE, JENNY AND I SPENT A lot of our time together while she picked my brain about the geography and animals of the Pacific Northwest. By now she was over her disappointment at how little I knew about Washington, DC.

"You know, Yankee, the *real* Washington."

She said she wanted to go to school in New York City, so we took trips over to the library and read magazines together about the Northeast. When we weren't at the library we'd sit on the porch swing and talk, or poke around the old Indian mound near the river, digging pottery fragments and occasional arrowheads from underneath the live oaks in the grove. Every day she said that she couldn't wait to get out of the South. Every day I wished I could figure out some way that I could stay.

When I found out that I was finally going to get my cast off I called her to share the good news.

"I haven't been able to get this arm wet for a month and I have to cover the cast every time I take a shower. It's been driving me crazy. So, here's an idea. I get it off next Tuesday morning; how about let's go over and just sit in the river for a while in the afternoon."

"Yankee, I'd love to but I'm fixin' to visit Daddy's sister and kids over by Waycross that week." She sighed. "You men. I swear y'all have the *worst* timing!"

I hung up, disappointed, and moped around the house until later in the day when I got a call from Mr. Yeomans. He said Jenny had talked about my getting the cast off, and since she wasn't going to be around I should come out and hunt up some new milkers with him. He said he'd carved another snake stick, a special one out of a seasoned yew branch, and did I want to try it out?

"You won't have to use your other hand much for what I have in mind; I need you mostly as a second pair of eyes so we can do a sweep of the property. I've been losing some chicks and I know the likely homes of a few of the resident snakes. Any big ones, we can save 'em for milking; take the rest over to the river. Deal?"

I didn't have to think for long. Ever since the accident I couldn't wrestle the lawnmower around and I was getting low on spending money.

"Yes, sir," I said. "Deal!"

The sky was dark and the wind was beginning to blow up hard the morning I got my cast off. By the time we got back from the hospital a tropical storm was hovering directly over us, pounding the county with rain. The storm lashed our house all day long and into the night, ripping palm fronds off the trees in the vacant lot across the street and overflowing the drainage ditch behind the house. The wind and rain finally died down the following morning, and when Mr. Yeomans picked me up the worst of the storm was rolling off into the northeast, accompanied by low grumbling thunder and occasional flashes of lightning. On the way out to the farm he drove slowly, his lights and wipers on, winding back and forth across the road to avoid the dark pools of standing water.

The bottom of the Yeomans' driveway had turned into a pond, and by the time I made it up onto the porch my tennis shoes were soaked through. Mr. Yeomans rummaged around in his kitchen closet and came up with an extra pair of waders. We picked our way south across the flooded orchard and through a stand of sugar pines to our starting point, a small lake on the back side of the property that was swollen by the heavy rain to twice its usual size.

For the next few hours we crisscrossed the property between the lake and the house, making the rounds of woodpiles and outbuildings and high ground, keeping one eye out for snakes and the other on the grey-black, muttering sky. By noon we had full bags: two large cottonmouths and a good-sized Eastern rattler, plus another smaller cottonmouth and one little coral. We slogged back to the trailer and housed the three big snakes in temporary cages, then took the little ones and released them over by the river.

"Give 'em a couple years to grow; we'll pick 'em up again," said Mr. Yeomans as we watched the two slither off into the undergrowth. The rain had started up again, a steady, sullen drizzle. "I'd say we're done. Let's go dry off and I'll drive you home."

The storm picked up again on our way, with rain falling in sheets and boiling black clouds filling the sky. Mr. Yeomans drove slowly and kept the lights on. By the time we got to our house the drainage ditch in front had overflowed and the yard had turned into a pond. I waded across and ran for the back porch, hugging the side of the house, but the slashing rain followed me under the eaves and by the time I made it to the back door I was completely soaked.

I stepped inside, stripped down to my shorts and was starting to hang things up to dry when there was a shriek from down the hall. I heard Mom scream, "Jesus Christ! Jesus Christ!", and a two-foot long cottonmouth came flying out of the laundry room, bounced off the hall wall and fell to the floor. I noticed in passing that it had one of Mom's bras in its mouth.

Mom was still screaming as the snake recovered and began to slither at top speed toward the front door, shaking its head from side to side and trying to dislodge the bra. I was frozen in place, and by the time I started to move the snake had freed itself, made it to the end of the hall and turned into the front room. There was a moment of silence, then a high, thin cry.

Oh, God, I thought. Mary.

I charged down the hall, still clutching my snake

stick. Mary was sitting in the corner to the left of the front door—the spot she typically shared with Cleo, a blanket, and her toys. She had her favorite cloth duck in one hand and part of the blanket in the other, and she was transfixed by the snake coiled directly in front of her. Cleo was at her side, hindquarters in the air, head and shoulders low to the ground. As I watched she slowly moved over to take a position between Mary and the snake. The snake lifted its head and flicked its tongue; Cleo bared her teeth and stood her ground, blocking the snake's path. The two swayed back and forth in unison, eyes locked.

I crept slowly into the room, got a good grip on the stick and swung, knocking the snake sideways. It bounced off the floor, recovered, and headed for the opposite corner of the room, but not quickly enough to escape. Cleo darted forward and sank her teeth in its body. The snake twisted backwards, burying its fangs in Cleo's shoulder. Cleo shook the snake back and forth, finally ripping its fangs from her shoulder, then she dropped the snake and ducked in to get a better grip just behind its head. I heard the crunch of teeth on bone as she broke its spine.

I tried to hook it away from her, but she turned and walked unsteadily over to the front door where she stood quietly, waiting. I tried again to make her to give up the snake but she just growled and held on. I finally opened the door and without a backward glance she stepped outside, plodded slowly across the grass toward the swamp and disappeared into the trees.

It took a while to calm Mom down and piece together what had happened. I figured the snake had come out of the swamp by way of the drainage ditch, looking for higher ground to wait out the storm. Getting into the laundry room would have been easy; it was just jerry-built off the back of the house with lots of cracks in the floor and walls. Mom said she had been pulling clothes out of the basket to put into the washer, and when she lifted some off the top of the pile she uncovered the snake. She pulled back just as it struck at her and caught its fangs in a bra she was holding, and her automatic reaction was to fling the clothing back over her head and out into the hall. The high-pitched scream I heard as the snake rounded the corner wasn't from Mary, it had come from Cleo – the first time she'd ever made a sound.

As soon as Jack and Martha got home I told them the story and the three of us went out to look for Cleo. We combed the neighborhood and the edges of the swamp for hours, but by dark she was still nowhere to be found. The next day Jack and I went door to door in the neighborhood, down the alleys and up in side yards, asking everyone if they had seen her. The story of her fight with the snake quickly spread through town and soon everyone was on the lookout.

On the third day there was still no sign of her.

On the morning of the fourth day I walked out the back door and almost tripped over her. She was curled up on the stairs, and except for looking a little thin she wasn't much the worse for wear. I carried her into the house, put her down next to Mary and brought her some food and water. She accepted these offerings in her usual regal manner, then curled up and went to sleep as if nothing had ever happened.

The only evidence of her run-in with the snake were two small puncture wounds in her shoulder which disappeared after a couple of days. When I told Mr. Yeomans about her miraculous recovery he said he wasn't really surprised; he figured the snake had exhausted most of its venom when it attacked Mom's underclothes. There hadn't been time for its poison sacs to refill, so Cleo only got a small dose when the snake bit her.

Cleo recovered fully in about a week and once again took up her job of guarding Mary full time. Mom put the bra in a sack and told me to throw it in the trash burner over behind the cabinet shop. We never found any trace of the snake.

## CHAPTER FORTY-SEVEN

THE DAY AFTER THE SNAKE GOT IN, JACK AND I SPENT ALL morning plugging cracks in the laundry room walls and floor. Mom was still shaken up, but now instead of being afraid she was just angry and more determined than ever to get us out of Georgia. We tried to point out the humor in what we called "The Great Snake and Bra Battle", but Mom wasn't having any of it. She saw the snake attack as an assault on her and her family, one more in a long line of indignities she'd suffered since arriving in the South. She'd been shunned for breast feeding baby Mary at Mass, ostracized by the neighbor ladies for being a Yankee, and humiliated when the other mill managers on Dad's level wouldn't invite us to their homes. For her, the snake incident was the last straw; the final reason to leave "this god-forsaken place". She didn't cut off my snake hunting and milking activities, but she did have me go out to the laundry room each morning and poke into all the corners with the snake stick before she went near the place. As an added precaution she brought my baseball bat in from the garage and leaned it up against the wall just inside the back door.

For about a week after the snake scare I didn't have much to occupy me. I had gotten used to spending a lot of time with Jenny, either at the library or out at her place, but she was still over in Waycross visiting her aunt and helping out with a new baby cousin. Louise had lost interest in me (and vice versa), Dal wasn't back yet from band camp, and Mr. Yeomans was doing some research with other university herpetologists over in Savannah, so I was left with time on my hands.

And not only was I bored, I was running low on money. My arm was still healing so I couldn't take the lawn mowing job back from Jack even if I had wanted to. And I really didn't want to; snake hunting was way more fun and it paid a lot more money. Of course, Mr. Yeomans had warned me about hunting alone, but I figured I knew enough and was careful enough that I could go after a few snakes on my own and have them ready for him when he got back. Besides, he had been complaining that he needed more milking stock. I decided to give my new snake stick a try.

I was squatting down in a ditch across from Jenny's place, trying to hook a medium-sized cottonmouth out of the undergrowth, when I heard a car approaching fast on the road above me. I stood up just in time to see Mr. Burroughs' Chevy flash past, and as it went by I could see the back of Dal's head in the passenger seat. The car drove on for a short distance, then slowed and turned in at the dirt path that led down to Mr. Burroughs' houseboat.

Dal. I'd been too embarrassed to tell him what Burroughs had tried to do to me. I'd thought about saying something but time went by and school let out; he was busy with the scouts and I was busy with the snakes and finally I just put it all aside. It was easier to ignore the incident, pretend it never happened. But now he was back from Band Camp, headed for Burroughs' houseboat and I had to figure out some way to warn him.

But how? I couldn't follow them down the path; there was no cover approaching the houseboat and Burroughs would be sure to see me. And as far as I knew there wasn't any other way in from the road.

I followed a rough animal trail toward the river, keeping a sharp eye out for snakes and, as I got closer to the river, alligators. The trail ended abruptly about a hundred yards downstream from the houseboat, on a bluff above a deep pool where the river made a tight loop and cut away at the sandy bank. It didn't look promising. I turned around, retraced my steps into the forest and ranged back and forth, looking for some other way through the trees and brush between me and the houseboat, but the area was completely covered with stinging nettles and firethorn. After a while I gave it up and went back out to the river bank. I peered down over the steep edge, measuring the distance to the water, and decided I'd rather chance that route than fight my way through the undergrowth. Some low-hanging vines got me most of the way down the ten-foot drop, but just as my feet touched the water the vines gave way and I plunged deep into a slow but powerful current. When I surfaced I grabbed some bushes along the bank while I caught my breath and watched my bag and snake stick float away.

I pulled myself along the bank into shallow water and then picked my way carefully upstream, fully expecting to see some snake drifting downriver toward me, eager to repay me for what I'd done to his relatives. Luckily none appeared. When I finally got to a piece of sandy shore I stripped naked, wrung out my pants and shirt, and emptied my shoes. Then I dressed again and made my way along the bank to another bend in the river where I could finally see the houseboat's roofline. A trail led up from the river to a clearing just across the slough from the houseboat, and at the edge of the clearing I could see through the picture window into the living room. One end of the big white sofa was visible between the partially opened curtains. I crouched down and waited for a minute, then moved crabwise across the clearing, staying low to the ground. I was almost to the other side when I looked up and froze in my tracks.

The whole sofa was now centered in the picture window, and Dal was bent over the far end of it. Mr. Burroughs was behind him, his eyes closed, his hands clutching Dal's hips, pushing violently into him again and again, each thrust rocking Dal's body back and forth. Dal's head was down, but before I could move again he looked up and our eyes met, and even from that distance I could see the tears streaming down his cheeks. He turned his face away; I stumbled across into the trees and ran.

## CHAPTER FORTY-EIGHT

THAT NIGHT I TOSSED AROUND IN BED UNTIL JACK FINALLY reached over and punched me.

"Goddamit, go to sleep or get the hell outta here! I got a game tomorrow!"

I picked up my clothes and climbed out the bedroom window into air that was still and heavy with moisture. A newly hatched crop of mosquitos swarmed me as soon as I got outside, but I hardly noticed their bites. Now I had two secrets to protect, mine and Dal's, and each time I tried to understand Dal's situation the possibilities got uglier. I needed to hear his story before I talked to anyone else.

I wandered the neighborhood until about two in the morning, trying to clear my head. Then I let myself back in the house and tried once again to sleep, lying still as a board so I didn't wake Jack, playing the scene at the houseboat over and over in my mind, not knowing what to do. I finally fell asleep at dawn. Mom shook me awake at eight and said I had a phone call.

"Will, it's Lorraine. Is Dal there?"

"No, ma'am. I haven't seen him today. Is he back now?" I heard the worry in her voice and felt sick that I couldn't be straight with her.

"Got back yesterday," she said. "Mr. Burroughs dropped him off at the house right when I was leaving for work. Said he had some things to do and took right off. I figured he'd be over to your place; you two not seeing each other for a whole week and all. That's okay, a course, it's just he always tells me if he's going to stay overnight."

I told her he hadn't been here and I didn't know where he was, but I promised to have him call home as soon as I saw him. I poked around the house all morning, then later in the afternoon I rode my bike over to his place, hoping I could find him and talk. The place was empty and the only sign of life was Boy wandering back and forth between the house and the old water tower.

His mom called a couple of times in the afternoon and once after dinner, asking if he'd shown up. She was starting to sound frantic.

## CHAPTER FORTY-NINE

BOY STARTED HOWLING ABOUT MIDNIGHT. HE KEPT IT UP, on and off, until daybreak, when one of the neighbors fought his way through the undergrowth by the water tower to see what all the noise was about. He found Boy lying patiently at the base of the tower, his head on his paws, guarding Dal's body. When the police came they had to throw a rope around Boy's neck and drag him away so they could get to Dal, who lay broken across the low concrete wall.

The coroner later concluded that he'd died instantly in the fall. The only thing of interest found during the autopsy was a tattered white square of cloth with a broken piece of twine attached, folded neatly and tucked into his back pocket.

## CHAPTER FIFTY

DAL FELL TO HIS DEATH ON MONDAY. FOR SOME REASON I expected the world to stop and take notice, but the world had its own ideas.

"Kids," Dad said as we all sat around the dinner table Wednesday night, "I know this has been a hard year for you, leaving Shelton and having to start a new school and, well, everything else." He looked around at us kids but nobody gave him much of a reaction. A lot of mealtime conversations had started this way; we were used to it. They weren't really conversations, more like pep talks—keep your spirits up, have faith in the future, God will provide. By now none of us expected anything different.

"Your mom and I have talked about this for a long time," Dad continued, "how Georgia just isn't the place for us, what with the Church and the weather and all and, well...I've decided to take another job."

The three of us stared at him.

"Up north."

Martha dropped her fork in her plate and put her hand over her mouth, her eyes wide.

"We'll be leaving in two weeks."

For the first time in months Dad was smiling and had some excitement in his voice; I didn't have to look at Mom to know how relieved she was. Jack and Martha and I interrupted each other as we swamped Dad with questions. Dad said his new mill was in a little town on the shores of Lake Michigan not far from Grand Rapids. The plan was for us to drive north, do some sightseeing along the way, and get there before the start of school. Mom and Dad were sensitive to Dal's death but there was still a lot to do before we left, so Mom pressed us all into action immediately, packing what was necessary for the trip and getting everything else boxed up for the movers. Martha made Dad and Mom both promise that, whatever else they left behind, Cleo was going with us.

Jenny was devastated when I told her. She retreated into herself, refusing to talk about Dal or about my leaving Yeomans. The few times I was able to get away and be with her there were huge silences between us. I was torn; I couldn't decide if I should tell her about Mr. Burroughs and me and Dal or just keep everything secret. In the end I decided to say nothing.

I was profoundly lonely. I didn't count many of the students as my friends, but if school had been in session at least we all could have stopped for a minute, crossing the schoolyard or in the cafeteria or class, to remember Dal together and share our grief. I finally realized just how exclusive my friendships with Dal and Jenny had been. They were the only ones who had really accepted me since I'd arrived, and I'd responded by insulating myself from almost everyone else. The only other person I had any connection to was Louise. After Dal's death I talked with her on the phone a few times, and I met her once downtown for a soft drink, but our silences were awkward and we really didn't have much to say to each other. I said my goodbyes to her long before we actually left Yeomans.

Dal's funeral took place at the end of summer vacation and the entire parish turned out to help support his mom. Father Donovan's sermon was both anguished and angry and I felt he was really close to questioning how God could allow such a death. I thought I saw him look at me when he talked about "dark forces in the world", but that might have just been my own guilt and confusion. Mr. Yeomans was still over at Savannah every weekend so Jenny came to the funeral alone. She arrived just before the service started, stood in the back of the church with her eyes down, and didn't talk with anyone. Judge came in a few minutes later and stood with her.

After the funeral everyone drove out to The Pig for barbecue. It was the first time I'd ever seen Judge pay attention to his mom. He brought her a plate of food and sat by her side with his arm around her, talking quietly. When lunch was over and the crowd was beginning to thin out I felt a heavy hand on my shoulder. I knew it was him even before I turned around.

"Hey, Yankee." I waited in the silence for him to say something else, but he just looked at me.

"Hey, Judge. I'm really sorry about Dal. I don't..." He cut me off.

"Yeah, we gotta talk about Dal. Tell your parents you're leaving for a bit; tell 'em I'll bring you home later." His hand had gone from resting on my shoulder to gripping it.

I checked in with Dad and said my condolences to Lorraine. Her face was gray with grief and she hardly acknowledged me, just closed her eyes, nodded, and patted me on the hand as I left. When I got out to Judge's car I found Jenny sitting in the back seat, a grim look on her face, and when I asked what was going on she just shook her head.

Judge drove us back to town without speaking and parked in front of Dal's house. After sitting for a minute in silence he reached into his pocket, unfolded a sheet of paper, and handed it to me. It was a note in Dal's handwriting that simply said, "Tell Will I'm sorry."

"I got a room down to the shop," said Judge, "so I don't come home much. But I was here this morning to get ready for the funeral and this was lying on my old dresser." His eyes were flat and hard. "What's this 'Tell Will I'm sorry' shit? What did he do? What's going on?"

I sat for a minute, searching for some words to explain. Then Jenny reached over the back of the seat and put her hand on my arm and said "Please," and the dam broke and I couldn't stop my tears. Everything poured out: fighting Burroughs off when he tried to molest me, seeing Dal being raped, trying to find him later and fearing what he would say, living with my shame for not saying something or asking for help. They didn't interrupt me but Jenny sobbed all the way through and once when I looked up I could see Judge's hands strangling the steering wheel. By the time I finished I was exhausted. Jenny leaned forward with her chin resting on my shoulder, my shirt damp with her tears. Judge just stared straight ahead.

"Anybody else know?"

"What? No, I don't know. If he never said anything to me or you guys, who would he tell?"

Judge pulled out a cigarette, lit it, and took a deep drag. He smoked in silence and when he was done he flicked the cigarette out the window and massaged his face with both hands. "Jesus Christ," he said. "What a fuckin' mess."

We sat and talked for a while, trying to come up with some sort of plan like going to the police or alerting the school or confronting Burroughs directly. The longer we talked the clearer it became that we couldn't prove anything, and finally Judge cut off the conversation.

"Yankee, Jenny said y'all are moving. Where y' going to?"

"Up north, somewhere in Michigan."

"When?"

"Next week, Saturday, I think. Why?"

He lit another cigarette and viciously shook out the match, his face grim.

"I don't know. I gotta think this through. This has gotta end up making sense somehow." He started the car and drove me home without another word.

## CHAPTER FIFTY-ONE

I WAS DOWN ON THE FLOOR BESIDE THE HIDE-A-BED, TRYING to wrestle my suitcase closed. We were leaving for Michigan in the morning and, except for having a few too many books for the trip to fit in my luggage, I was done packing. I shifted all my weight to one knee and got one of the clasps to click shut, then took a breather and looked out across the living room. We'd packed up the moving van the day before so except for a blanket and some toys left out for Mary and Cleo, the room was empty. I had the strange feeling of going back in time and seeing the house that first moment I walked through the front door, almost as if the last twelve months hadn't happened at all. I sighed. There were so many reasons I wished they hadn't.

"Will! Jenny on the phone!" This was a surprise; I'd said my goodbyes to her the day before when I went out to collect my last payment from her dad. She was as distant then as she had been at the funeral. When I was ready to leave she had given me a distracted hug, and when I tried to kiss her goodbye she turned her head and pulled away and said only that she'd be in touch.

I stopped fighting with the suitcase and ran back to the kitchen. Mom was supervising Martha in a full-house deep cleaning which included the stove; I stretched the phone's long cord out into the hall to get some privacy. Jenny's voice sounded urgent.

"Will, we need your help."

"Uh, okay. What's...?"

"I can't explain now but we don't have much time and this is really important. Just tell me if you can get away after dinner for about an hour. Please?"

"I guess so. What's...?" I heard her say "Bye!" and the line went dead.

It was almost dark by the time she and Judge showed up. Mom was busy getting Mary to bed and Martha and Jack still had some packing to do, so I wasn't going to be missed; I slipped out with a quick, "Back in a sec!" and jumped in the car. As soon as he drove away Judge said, "We need a snake."

"You what? Why?"

"Never mind. We need a snake. Tonight. Jenny's Dad's over in Savannah and he's comin' back tomorrow afternoon late so it has to be tonight."

"Why? I need to know..."

"No." Judge cut me off. "You don't."

I turned around and looked at Jenny. She had folded herself into the corner of the back seat with her arms around her legs. She looked very small and scared.

"Okay," I said, "This is crazy. Jenny, you and I both

know where the trailer key is. Either of us could get in there, but your Dad will know it wasn't you. You're too damn afraid of snakes. I'm the only one who knows how to handle one, so who's he gonna suspect? What're you guys asking me to do?"

Judge took his eyes off the road for a moment to look at me; his face was hard. "I can't tell you why but you gotta do this. I'll protect you, Yankee; no one's ever gonna know you had anything to do with...anything. But I swear to God I'll hurt you if you don't help us."

We rode the rest of the way to Jenny's house in silence. As we turned into the driveway our headlights illuminated the old weeping willows, their branches casting sharp shadows against the farmhouse and the trailer beyond. Old Major was in the kitchen but he heard the crunch of tires and set up a mournful howl. Judge stopped down at the end of the driveway and turned out the lights. We sat in the darkness and I thought about what they were asking for. I didn't like it at all.

"So, you won't tell me what you're up to?"

"Nope."

"Okay, okay. What kind of snake?"

"Whaddaya mean? Those ones you milk, they're all poisonous, right?"

"Yeah, but the cottonmouths and rattlers mostly make you real sick; the coral's the only one that's guaranteed to kill you."

"That one," Judge said, without hesitation.

Oh, Christ, I thought.

I got out of the car and walked around the corner of the house to the trailer. I tried the old double-hung windows and the front door. Locked tight. After a minute Jenny brought me the key from the kitchen and then went back to sit in the darkened car. I stared at the trailer, at its front door with the large, single pane window, then I walked back to the car and tossed the key to Jenny in the back seat.

"Okay, here's what we need to do."

When I was finished Judge looked over at Jenny and said "Sounds good." She nodded. He got out and followed me back to the trailer to act as a lookout. When we got there I folded my light jacket, placed it up against the window in the trailer door and drove my fist through it. Glass tinkled to the floor. I reached inside, twisted the deadbolt lock and opened the door.

When I flicked on the overhead lights every snake was at full alert, their heads turning to follow me as I crossed the room. I found the coral snake's glass cage up on a high shelf and brought it down to the table. The snake was used to being handled, so the transfer into the bag took only a few seconds. I cinched the bag tight and set it down, then rifled through the drawer of snake milking paraphernalia, dumping the contents across the table and onto the floor. I dragged a cottonmouth's cage across the room and left it just inside the door. I surveyed the scene from the doorway, then I went back, lifted the coral snake's cage, and threw it against the wall. The glass exploded, the metal lid bounced off into a far corner, and inside the house Old Major began to howl. I grabbed the bag, flicked off the light, and ran to the car.

## CHAPTER FIFTY-TWO

"JACK, WILL; LAST CHANCE! ANYTHING YOU CAN'T FIND just leave it, we've got a full day ahead!"

We closed up the house and took one last drive through town. Our first stop was The Pig, for their all-you-can-eat family style brunch. It was the sort of meal that Mom would never let us have on a normal day because of all the fat and calories, but it was perfect for the start of a long road trip. I piled my plate with eggs, boiled okra, grits, potatoes, fried green tomatoes and sausage patties, all heavily salted and dripping with grease. Even Mom went back for seconds. I looked around for Dal's mom but the manager said she was taking some time off and wouldn't be in until the following week. On our way out Jack and I made a quick stop at the alligator pond, but there weren't any chicks for sale in the gift shop and we couldn't get a rise out of the reptiles.

The last stop was St. Jude's. Mom insisted that we all go to Confession on our way out of town, pointing out that we were starting a long trip filled with danger and uncertainty, and if we all perished in a fiery crash (her words) at least we would die in a State of Grace. We kids reminded her that she'd already equipped the car with a new St. Christopher (Patron Saint of Travelers!) medal and that should be enough protection. But we were overruled, and at two o'clock we were first in line at church as Father Donovan entered the Confessional. I let the rest of the family go ahead and lingered in the pew, trying to decide what I was going to say. When it came my turn I still hadn't come up with an answer.

"Bless me, Father, for I have sinned."

I hadn't been to Confession since before Dal's death, before I saw him and Mr. Burroughs on the houseboat. I was still trying to understand my part in all of it and what, if any, responsibility I had. I'd witnessed an evil act, a crime against my best friend, and I hadn't done anything about it. I knew what I'd seen but I didn't know the truth behind it. Was it the first time Dal had been with Mr. Burroughs? If not, how long had it been going on, and how did I know that Dal wasn't a willing participant? It made me sick to think about him that way, but I just didn't know anything for sure any more. And even if Dal had been a complete victim I couldn't prove it to anyone. He was dead, Burroughs was alive, and I was the only person who had seen anything.

"Yes, son?"

"Just a second, Father."

If I wasn't going to say anything about Dal, what was I doing here? What else had I done lately that really needed absolution? I could almost predict the conversation:

*"Bless me, Father, for I have sinned; my last confession was two weeks ago. I stole a snake."*

*"A snake."*

*"Yes, Father."*

*"A snake. Why did you steal a snake?"*

*"Um, I can't really say, Father."*

*"Okay, was this a prank, then?"*

*"Well, no..."*

I sat there, knowing I couldn't have that conversation. Father Donovan's voice broke in again on my thoughts.

"Son, are you there? Son?" I leaned in close to the screen and lowered my voice.

"Father, I know you can't give me absolution for something I don't confess. I can't tell you anything right now but I just want to say I'm sorry. I'm sorry and I need you to pray for me."

I didn't wait for his response. I walked out of the confessional, out of the church, out into the hard Georgia sunshine where my family was waiting.

It was going to be a long trip.

---

## CHAPTER FIFTY-THREE

"SIR? SIR, PLEASE WAKE UP."

I opened my eyes. Leaning over me was the night nurse who had given me coffee and the blanket.

"It's the Judge, sir. He's awake; he wants to talk with you." I stood up and stretched and listened for the owl, but outside the forest was quiet and the darkness was complete.

When I got to the room Judge was propped up a little straighter in bed. He motioned me to come in.

"They finally gave me a big enough dose to knock back the pain. Pull that chair up and gimme some more water. This is gonna take a while." He clutched the glass I gave him and I could see the backs of his sinewy hands, bruised blue and yellow from the injections. He took a deep breath and coughed, a hollow, racking sound.

"First of all, I gotta take responsibility for a lot of what happened." He saw the surprise on my face and waved me off when I tried to speak. "Don't interrupt. It's a long story." He coughed again and wiped his mouth with the edge of the sheet. I saw flecks of blood, black in the dim lamplight.

"Okay, gotta go back a while for this to make sense. First off, I knew about Burroughs before you did. Our daddy had left and we had some real hard times for a couple years, before Ma started workin' for The Pig. She got involved with the church, lookin' for support, and Burroughs was right there to offer it. He was always hangin' around, bein' sweet to her and me and Dal, and she never knew what else he was doin'. Right after he made his move on me I just up and left home; never told her why and never told anyone else, either. I couldn't. Burroughs was quality around here, had an in with the clergy and the folks that ran the town. Besides, I was just a kid and usually in some kind of trouble. No one was gonna believe me if I said anything." He finished the water. I poured a refill and waited for him to get his breathing under control.

"I guess I knew he might try the same with Dal, but Dal never said anything and I just didn't want to think about it. I didn't put it all together 'til the police found him by the water tower." He was quiet for a moment. "You know he didn't fall, right?"

"What? No." I shook my head. "I don't get it."

"Remember when you fell? You hit the walkway and one of the planks gave out and you came straight down, landed a couple feet inside that little concrete wall. Didn't happen that way with Dal. He landed right on the wall, broke his back. I figured the only way he could get out far enough to hit the thing was to jump. I think the priest knew it too but he didn't say; that way Dal could be buried from the church. Would've killed Ma otherwise. Anyway, when you told us what Burroughs did to you and Dal, I just decided to finish things, make up for my part in it somehow." He smiled grimly. "You did a good job with your part, Yankee; getting' that snake."

I felt the familiar clenching in my stomach, remembering that night at the trailer. I nodded and waited for him to go on.

"Okay. Right after we dropped you off that night Jenny and I drove out to Burroughs' place. She stayed with the car and I went down to the boat, looked through the window. Burroughs was sittin' in there, reading. I waited a few minutes 'til I was sure nobody else was around. Then I went and knocked on the door, and when he opened up...I just lost it. I only hit him once and he went right down. I really wanted to beat him to death but there would've been too much blood." He grimaced and took a few deep breaths and that started the coughing again. I handed over the water. This time it took longer for him to get control.

"I stood over him and thought of all those years... How many kids besides me and Dal..." His voice trailed off as another coughing fit took over. When he was done he raised his hand and motioned me in closer.

"So, I had duct tape and the snake bag. I gagged him and rolled him on his stomach, taped his hands behind him, jammed his head inside the bag and pulled back on the cords, hard as I could. Never been so scared in my life. When he came to he started thrashing around and that's when the snake got him. I heard him tryin' to scream, but I just sat on him and rode it out. Took a long time 'til he got quiet.

His voice was getting weaker. I asked if he wanted to rest but he shook his head.

"Anyway, I went outside and untied his canoe and kicked it out into the current, then I dragged him out on the path and closed the place up. Next part was the hardest. I yanked the bag off his head and the fuckin' snake took off like a shot toward the river. God, I never wanted to see another snake again in my life." He lay back and closed his eyes for a few minutes.

"When I picked him up he was still breathing and moving around some. Never figured he'd still be alive. Son of a bitch, you said the coral was the deadliest snake and here Burroughs wasn't dead; I think I would'a killed you right then if I could've. So I dragged him to the car and Jenny helped me get him in the trunk. She said later she damn near lost her mind waitin' for me up at the road, duckin' down every time someone drove by, thinkin' they were gonna stop. Anyhow, I knew a big gator hole way back in the swamp, up where the Oconee and the Altamaha come together. When we got there I weighed Burroughs down with some scrap metal from the shop and dropped him in near the undercut and we backed into some bushes and waited. About daylight a big old gator showed up draggin' the body, at least I thought I saw an arm or something in his mouth when he went by. So we waited and waited and finally just came home. Jesus, it was months before I stopped looking over my shoulder, worrying that the gator hadn't finished the job, that somehow Burroughs'd surface and I'd get caught."

I started to speak. Judge lifted a hand to cut me off and closed his eyes, talked out for the moment. I leaned back in the chair and thought about what I'd done. The coral snake had been big, the biggest one I'd ever seen. I knew from working with Mr. Yeomans that its bite would be fatal; that's what Judge wanted, that's why I selected it. But I never thought any further than that. I never had any reason to think that Burroughs might end up being dropped in the river alive. Now I knew the rest of the story. Was this the justice I'd been looking for?

After a few minutes I opened my eyes to find Judge looking at me, a tired, tight smile on his face.

"That's all I got, Yankee. No more secrets. Any questions?"

"So how'd you find me? And why send me that letter now?"

"Oh, that was easy. Jenny was a whiz with the internet, always knew where you were and what you were up to. Even pulled up some of your online papers about child abuse; said they were pretty good, too. She said you deserved to know how this all played out. We just had to time it right."

"What?"

"Murder's a capital crime, Yankee. Anybody dug deep enough into this and found out what really happened they could tag you as an accessory. And there's no statute of limitations. But Jenny's gone and I'll be dead soon so you're the only person who knows anything about this, the only witness. And I owed you. I always felt guilty I wasn't there for Dal, and you were a friend to him in a way I couldn't be. I just thought it'd be good if you didn't have to carry this load of shit around anymore."

## CHAPTER FIFTY-FOUR

THE NURSING STAFF TRIED TO KICK ME OUT AT SHIFT CHANGE but Judge told them to leave us the hell alone except when he needed something for the pain. He dozed on and off through the night and when he slept I slept too, but when he was awake he wanted to talk. And he talked about everything: growing up with Dal, overcoming poverty, building his business and his reputation in the community, Jenny.

"Jenny, she always wanted more than just Yeomans; I guess I oughta thank you for that. Or maybe blame you. You were the first person she ever met that wasn't from here. She wanted what it looked like you had. Me, I was never much for traveling..."

They dated on and off through high school; he wanted to get married, she couldn't make up her mind. Then right after graduation she left for the University of Georgia, got a degree in marine biology and started her teaching career. She only came back to Yeomans for a short time in the early '90s, when her dad had a stroke. She nursed him until he died, then sold the farm and went off to teach in upstate New York. She never came back.

"We always kept in touch. I got married, got divorced, but we still kept writing. When she got diagnosed she wanted to get you some closure on Burroughs. I did too but we had to be careful; had to time it right so nobody got caught, like in some cold case murder mystery. So after she died and I got sick I figured it was time. Here, gimme a hand."

He leaned forward so I could get under his arms. I pulled him up in the bed and rearranged the pillows behind him, amazed at how little he weighed. He leaned back and closed his eyes against the pain. After a few minutes his breathing eased into sleep. I grabbed a stray pillow for my head and curled up in the chair.

Toward morning I woke up to the sound of his cough.

"Hey, Yankee, remember the car?"

"The Grey Ghost? Yeah, why?"

"Turn on the light for a second. Pull out the drawer over there by you, over on that table. Check out the matches."

I fished in the drawer. There was a pack of unfiltered Camels and a couple of matchbooks with "Grey Ghost Garage" on the front, the words arching over a monochrome drawing of his 1950 Chevy Fleetline.

"You smoke? Well, take 'em anyways, y'never know."

He'd worked at the repair shop until he had enough money to buy the place from his boss. Eventually he owned two shops, one in Yeomans and one at the other side of the county, over in McRae. He said that had kept him more than busy, along with all the political stuff. A memory clicked in my head.

"Dal started to tell me something the first time we met, started to say why they called you Judge." There was a soft chuckle and another cough.

"When I was a kid somebody started a rumor that our mother screwed around with a local judge before she had me. Never knew if it was true but I beat the shit out of the kid that said it. Anyhow, the name stuck. I got to be kind of a Robin Hood type, just not the stealing part. I'd get mad if I saw kids being picked on, pushed around; I'd step in and settle things. Believe me, you'da had a lot more fights on your hands if I hadn't been around." His voice trailed off and he paused to get his breath. "Funny thing is, I *am* a judge now. Got elected to the County here twenty years ago; haven't lost an election since."

He drifted off again. I leaned back in my chair and looked out the window toward the east. In the dawn, streamers of blue and pink and gold stretched out across the sky and found their way into the room. I closed my eyes and drifted off to the faint sounds of music, the low rumble of French horns and saxophones and the clear, bright notes of the clarinets, all working their way slowly toward sunrise.

I woke when an aide pushed a steam cart into the room, followed by a nurse to check on Judge. When he didn't wake up I wandered on out to the porch and sat for a while, watching the early sun chase shadows over the rolling hills. At eight o'clock, my cell phone buzzed with a text: "Up early. Missing you. R." I smiled and typed in, "Miss you too. Back soon with some good news."

I tried to feed Judge when he woke up but all he wanted was a little water, and after I gave it to him he slipped back into unconsciousness. I sat by his bed for a while, drank a cup of coffee, and ate a piece of toast from his tray. He was still sleeping when I finished. I looked at his sunken face and tried to remember him when we were kids and wished I could redo the years in between. Finally I reached out and took his hand.

"Gotta go, Judge. Got a couple of things to do before the flight."

"Thanks, Yankee," he whispered, his eyes still closed. I waited for something more but that was all. He squeezed my hand for the last time.

## CHAPTER FIFTY-FIVE

THE OLD YEOMANS PLACE WAS IN BETTER SHAPE THAN I HAD ever seen it: new paint, well-trimmed lawn and garden, and a row of dwarf peach and apple trees running along the fence. I drove toward the end of the property and parked across the road under a canopy of oak trees. Late Sunday morning in a God-fearing, churchgoing Southern town, I thought. There wouldn't be much traffic.

I left the car in the shadows and walked down the road toward the airport. Fifty years earlier the path to Burroughs' houseboat had been easy to find; now it was all but invisible, not much more than a faint trail blocked with brush and hanging vines. I plunged in and fought my way through the undergrowth, swatting at the mosquitos and keeping an eye out for snakes. I was just about ready to give up when I caught a glimpse of weathered metal roofing off to the right. I pushed on. After a few more minutes I broke free of the tangled foliage and found myself standing at the top of a sandy bluff.

The river had disappeared. The channel where it used to flow was now a wide, shallow ditch filled with palmettos, live oaks, and sugar pines. Burroughs' houseboat lay up against the near side of the ditch, her deck tilted at an angle. I picked my way down the slope through weeds and blackberry vines to a makeshift ladder of two-by-fours leaning up against the boat, then pulled myself up past the broken railing and onto the deck. The picture window through which I'd last seen Dal was long since gone, the glass shattered and scattered. I stepped through the window, through the kudzu and dusty wild clematis that filled the frame. The curtain of vegetation closed behind me. I felt around in my pocket and found one of Judge's matchbooks.

The flame from the match showed a scene of total destruction. Windows were smashed, the ceiling sagged, holes were punched in the sheetrock, and inside the holes I could see a tangled ruin of insulation and wiring. There was a moldy, bitter smell in the air; the scent of rodents and urine and worse. The huge white couch still occupied the center of the room but the plush pillows were gone, and one arm of the couch was ripped partly off. It hung, like a broken wing, parallel to the floor. The back of the couch had been sliced open diagonally and its stuffing scattered.

The match flickered and went out. Sunlight filtered through the shroud of vines and shadows moved against the back wall. I could hear a faint scratching sound from the corner of the room as I stood for a moment in the dim light, remembering the last time I'd been inside the place.

I lit another match. The wall-to-wall carpet was dotted with cigarette holes. Half a century of wear had turned it a mottled grey except for one area directly in front of the couch; a darker, greyish-pink stain. I bent over for a closer look and the memories came rushing back: the sweet cloying taste of sloe gin, the stink of Burroughs' breath, my unexpected fountain of vomit arcing into his face and splashing in a red puddle on the rug. I tasted bile in my throat and closed my eyes and the images continued. I saw Dal bending over the couch, looking straight at me; his coffin standing alone on the empty altar; his mom's shattered face as she sat in the condolence line in the church hall, holding a paper plate of food and trying to comprehend what had happened to her life.

The match burned down to my fingers and I dropped it on the floor. I stood in the dark, in the middle of the wreckage the houseboat had become, thinking about Burroughs and all the people he'd damaged and how I'd never get the chance to piss on his grave, and in the quiet shadows I said goodbye to Dal and Jenny and Judge.

I wiped my face dry with my sleeve and lit another match.

## CHAPTER FIFTY-SIX

THE GROUND CREW HAD ALREADY STARTED TO PULL BACK the rolling stairs when I came sprinting across the tarmac. I made it on board and found my seat and strapped in under the disapproving eye of the stewardess. Then we taxied, turned, and sat a moment before the pilot released the brakes and the small plane gathered speed down the runway and lifted off.

I looked out the window. A couple miles away, where Burroughs' houseboat sat in the former river channel, a tall plume of black smoke rose slowly in the still morning air. It pushed straight up until it hit the prevailing winds, then flattened out and drifted off to the west. Down on the highway I could see flashing blue and red lights as a line of fire trucks and emergency vehicles sped out from town, heading toward the smoke.

The plane banked sharply and we headed north to

Atlanta. I looked at Rebekkah's text once again and smiled, thinking about her voice, her lips next to my ear, her mouth on mine. I closed my eyes and settled in for the long flight home.

*- end -*

MICHAEL DESCAMP IS A NATIVE OF THE PACIFIC NORTH-west who, after a lifetime of writing, brings out his debut novel at the age of seventy-four. Some authors are just faster than others.

In addition to the usual education and work history, Michael survived growing up with eight siblings in the Deep South, flew seventy-two combat missions in Viet Nam, managed a surfing hotel in Mexico, and now spends his winters in South Africa with his wife Jackie.

Michael lives most of the time in Portland, Oregon with Jackie and their granddog Murray (when they can wrestle him away from the kids). You can check out his blog at mikedescamp.com and correspond at mikedescamp@gmail.com.

CPSIA information can be obtained
at www.ICGtesting.com
Printed in the USA
BVHW071109230719
554154BV00001B/38/P